Dealing with Malice

The Saga of Tobias Crow

Book 2

P.S. Osborne

This is a work of fiction. Names, characters, businesses, places, events, locales, and incidents are either the products of the author's imagination or used in a fictitious manner. Any resemblance to actual persons, living or dead, or actual events is purely coincidental.

First Edition
Published 2022

Copyright ©2022 by Paul Osborne
All Rights Reserved. No part of this publication may be reproduced, stored in a retrieval system, or transmitted, in any form or by any means, electronic, mechanical, photocopying, recording, or otherwise, without the prior written permission of the publisher.

P.S. Osborne asserts his moral right to be identified as the author of this work.

ISBN: 9798843282912

Dedication

To my Dad who I am sure was driven to near insanity by my fevered imagination when I was growing up. I know that he would be immensely proud to see the same imagination which made me such a handful as a child, become something constructive as ~~an adult~~ a bigger child.

I miss him deeply and he is always in my thoughts.

Chapter 1

There is no such thing as monsters.

That is what we tell ourselves. It is what our parents assured us each and every night that we were too afraid to sleep. All those things that we fear, all the things that go bump in the night and hide in the darkness just outside our windows, they are all just figments of our imaginations. None of them really exist and there is nothing to be afraid of.

We keep telling ourselves this, but do we ever truly believe it?

Tobias Crow didn't. He had always known that monsters were real. He had seen them. He had survived several long days of torment and terror in their domain. And though he had escaped, the memories of the ordeal were still fresh and festering deep inside him.

The nightmares were the worst. They had become a regular occurrence in Tobias' life and though they wouldn't always be clear, they were always there. They crept in each night and caused him to wake every morning in a cold sweat.

That morning, the nightmare from which he woke was a particularly vivid one. One which felt real enough that he couldn't be certain where the dream ended and the real world began. It lingered in his mind like a sinister echo.

He was outside the apartment block where he lived. The featureless grey building loomed up behind him and the street stretched out like a glistening river of tarmac. Yet nothing else looked familiar. The houses which lined the road were shrouded in darkness, and all the colour of the world was muted, as if a fine black gauze had been draped over the entire scene. Even the sky was a solid, inky black without a single star or speck of moon to break up the smooth emptiness.

Tobias looked around for any signs of life. There were no lights on in the windows, no people peering out from their doors, not even a dog barking in the distance. It was pure silence. The kind of unnatural silence that could not occur in the waking world, but which amplified the sense of isolation Tobias now felt. He opened his mouth to shout but no sound emerged.

A chill ran up his spine, causing him to turn sharply on the spot. Walking slowly up the street towards where he now stood was a lean figure with pure white skin and wearing a dark grey robe. Its hood was up over its head but was pushed back just enough so the face was visible. At least, its face would have been visible if it had one. The porcelain skin was unblemished by features of any kind. No nose, mouth, or even eyes. There was nothing to produce any expression, and Tobias had nothing with which he could judge its intent.

Tobias turned his attention from the featureless head to the figure's clenched hands. Both were stained crimson by a wet, tacky liquid which seeped out from between the fingers and dripped onto the floor. It left two long trails of splatter as the figure walked with purpose straight towards Tobias.

There was an urge to run. A desperate need to flee from this strange creature which was approaching with ominous intent. But Tobias muscles would not respond. No matter how hard he tried, he just could not get his legs to move. All he could do was watch as the thing creeped ever closer.

Its head tilted to one side and its hands began to pulse as more and more of the viscous fluid ebbed out. Soon it was too late for Tobias to do anything but watch. The thing was already too close to escape. It reached towards Tobias' face and its hands opened.

Within the swollen flesh of its palms were two grotesque and gaping mouths, bristling with thousands of tiny, needle-like fangs. The maws frothed and foamed with blood.

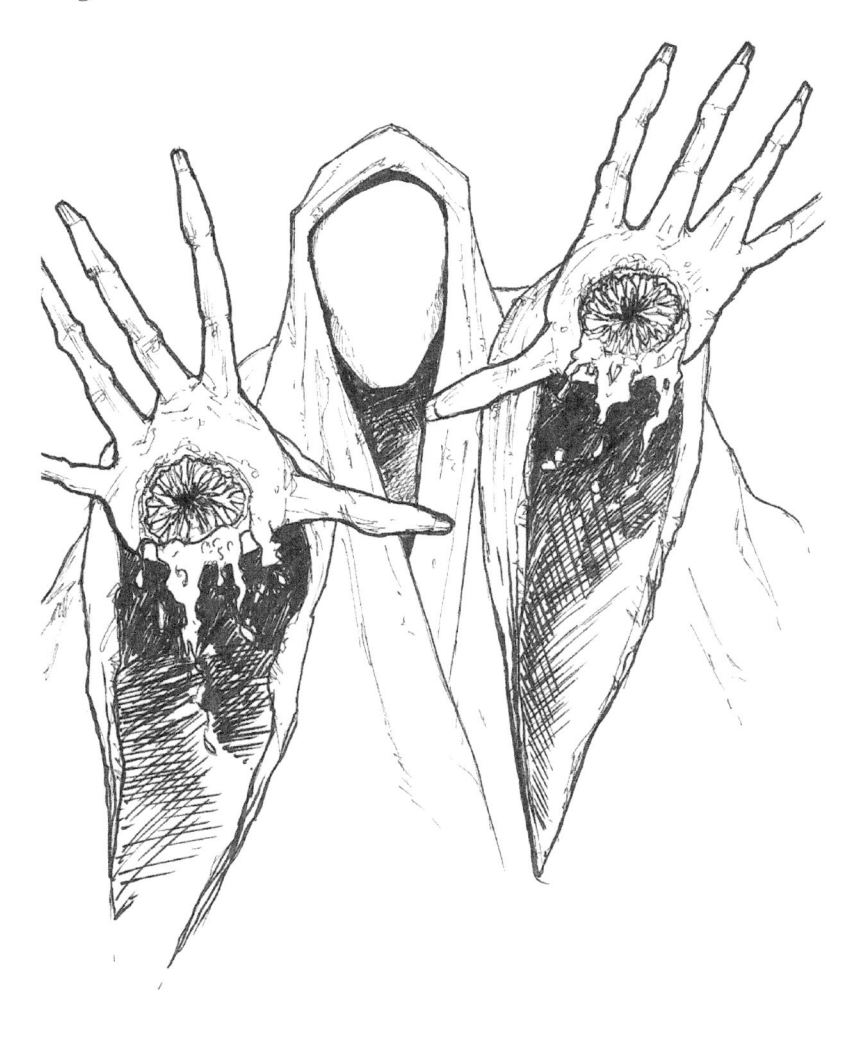

Tobias tried to scream again but still no sound emerged as the hands clasped around his face and the mouths bit deep into the flesh of his eyes.

That was when Tobias woke, panting and sweating in his bed. Nightmares were a curse he had not been able to shake, but it was a curse he had become accustomed to. Despite this, it was the first time this horrific, faceless creature had appeared in his dreams, and Tobias did what he had always done when presented with something new and terrifying, he named it. It took him only the briefest flash of a second to decide on *The Stranger*, and then, with a name chosen and the fear lessened, he tried to put it to the back of his mind.

After taking a moment to catch his breath, Tobias pulled himself out from beneath his cold, damp sheets and set about preparing himself for the day. He pulled away the stool which blocked his wardrobe door each night and retrieved some clothes. There wasn't a lot of choice but he still took some time deciding before settling on a simple grey t-shirt and some jeans. Once dressed he moved over and looked at himself in the mirror which hung on the back of his bedroom door.

With yet another nightmare still fresh in his mind, he couldn't help but think about what was lurking deep down inside him.

On the surface, he looked like a rather normal young boy. His thirteenth birthday was just two months away and despite being small for his age, he was beginning to bulk out. His hair was a messy tangle of brown perched on top of his head and his green eyes betrayed nothing of the darkness which stirred deep down in his soul. But he knew better.

Coiled within him was a soul fragment belonging to a creature of immense power, and even greater evil. For the last few years everything in Tobias' life had been shaped by this dark presence. It was the reason his parents had died when he was six, and it was the reason he had found himself in the care of his drunk and abusive uncle, consigned to a life of misery.

For six years, Tobias had lived a life of terror and hardship without ever knowing the truth of what lay dormant inside. That was until Tobias' ordeals in the Underlands.

Four months had passed since Tobias had escaped the twisting stone passages of that realm, and his thoughts regularly drifted back to the horrors which he had faced there. Both the vile creatures that he had battled, and the dark secrets which he had learned. In the depths of the Underlands, the taint that was Tyringar had awoken from its slumber and was now an ever present clawing at the back of his mind. A hard knot of anger and hatred which never abated.

He closed his eyes tight and cleared his mind. Such thoughts were not welcome. They crept in whenever he let his mind wander, but he was getting better at blocking them out. He had suffered, but he had also emerged from this ordeal harder, stronger and with power over his fears. He had battled the darkness and he had survived.

Reaching up, he brushed his fingers over a small faded photo taped to the top corner of the mirror. Most of the colour had gone now, but the joy of the image remained untarnished. His parents, happy and beautiful, walking out from a church into a cheering crowd. It was a reminder of how life should have been.

Tobias kissed his fingers and pressed them to the picture. A smile crept its way to his face. It was a sad smile, but a smile none-the-less. It was the smile that always came when he was forced to think of everything he could have had. Especially when compared to what he now lived with.

The smile was never alone either. It was always accompanied by an involuntary glance downwards. A glance which forced him to acknowledge the object which now hung on his door handle and caused his mind to real with conflicting emotions.

Like him, the object looked unassuming. Just a plain leather cord which wrapped its way around a purple teardrop stone. Also like him, the object was not entirely what it seemed.

Shimmering as the light caught it's surface, the stone was in fact a clear glass-like material, and beneath its polished surface, purple smoke churned in lazy, ever shifting patterns. This was Hexalbion. A companion with whom Tobias had escaped the Underlands. A trapped soul, bound in the stone and tormented by his past deeds. Deeds which included the death of Tobias' parents.

Reaching for the stone with trembling fingers, Tobias stopped himself just short of actually touching it. He let his arm drop back to his side and returned to his bed.

'You can't keep ignoring me,' said the raspy voice of the stone as Tobias walked away.

Tobias flopped down on his mattress and laid, staring up at the ceiling.

'Please believe me,' Hex continued. 'If I could go back and change what I did, I would do it in an instant.'

'I'm sorry Hex. I do forgive you, but it's hard to just forget what happened.'

'I would never expect you to forget. I did a terrible thing.'

'You didn't have a choice,' Tobias replied, but even he thought it sounded unconvincing.

'I did have a choice. I could have refused as soon as the Witch Mother commanded me, but I was a coward.'

'I don't blame you Hex.' Tobias said wearily.

'Then why are you still punishing me? I have been stuck in this room for months, just hanging here like a glorified decoration. I want to be out.'

Tobias felt a hint of anger rising in his gut. 'Is that what this is all about?' He snapped. 'All this regret? It's just to get me to take you out?'

'No, of course not, but you did promise to free me and so far all you have done is dump me here.'

'I said I would free you and I will.'

'When?'

'How am I meant to know? It's not like you've come up with any ideas on how I'm supposed to do it.'

'How would you know what ideas I have?' Hex spat back. His anger was rising too. 'You never ask me. You barely even talk to me. You have got what you wanted and now you couldn't care less about the rest of us.'

Enraged by Hex's words, Tobias shot to his feet and stormed over to the stone.

'Got what I wanted?' He yelled. 'How have I got what I wanted? My parents are still dead!'

He snatched Hex off from the door handle and hurled him across the room into the cupboard.

'Tobias, I'm sorry, I didn't mean to…'

Hex's words were cut off as the door slammed shut.

Tobias clenched his fists tight at his side and took a deep breath. The anger at the back of his mind was growing and he knew he needed to get control. Breathing out slowly, he let his muscles relax and his body slump slightly. Then he sat back on the edge of his bed and looked down at the green blanket at his feet. The mound of cloth shifted slightly as something beneath stirred into life. Slowly the blanket began to rise and stretch before parting to reveal a small bat-like snout which sniffed tentatively at the air.

'It's okay,' Tobias said to the creature as it slowly pulled itself free and hopped over to his lap.

Scavenger had always been a chubby little creature with a hairless body covered in folds of wrinkled flesh, but since leaving the underlands he had put on even more weight. His bony arms and long rat-like tail had bulked out to match his already powerful back legs. Even his flat nosed face was starting to look rather round and pudgy. Tobias had contemplated putting him on a diet, but simply hadn't had the heart. Scavenger loved his food far too much.

'Do you think I was too hard on Hex?' Tobias asked as he scratched Scavenger behind one of his large ears.

Scavenger looked up at him with a slight tilt of the head and a blank stare. The ear Tobias was scratching was perked up straight while the other hung limp, covering one of his eyes.

'I don't hate him,' Tobias continued, as much to himself as to the rodent. 'I just don't know if I can forget the part he played in everything.'

Scavenger squeaked and curled up into a small wrinkly ball.

'Maybe I do need to go easier on him.'

Tobias repositioned Scavenger on the edge of the bed and laid down next to him

'I'm glad you're here,' Tobias said as he cuddled Scavenger in tight. 'Hex is trying to help, and my uncle's getting better, but it still feels like without you, I would be all alone. Do you know what I mean?'

Scavenger didn't reply. Instead he wriggled his chubby hairless body until it was comfortably squashed into the space under Tobias arm and then began to snore.

Chapter 2

Tobias didn't move for nearly an hour. He just laid on his bed, cuddling Scavenger and staring at the ceiling. He told himself it was because he didn't want to wake his friend, but when Scavenger eventually started to disturb, Tobias still didn't feel ready to get up. He tried his best to ignore the wriggling movements of his friend, but was eventually forced to give in when Scavenger pawed at his shoulder and nuzzled into his cheek, all culminating in a wet snorting noise in his ear.

'Are you getting hungry?' Tobias asked.

In response Scavenger squeaked loudly before jumping down from the bed and rushing over to the bedroom door. He spun around in several circles before looking back at Tobias and squeaking again.

'Okay, okay. I'm coming.'

Tobias eased himself out of bed, and pulling the door open, he followed Scavenger out into the main room of the apartment. It had changed a lot over the previous four months. The whole room had benefited from a full clean and redecoration with much of the old furniture being thrown away. Even his uncle's armchair, which had always reeked of the man's stale sweat and filth, had been replaced with a new leather sofa bought from the local charity shop.

The only thing that remained of the old room was the small brown television. The plan was to replace that too, but other costs had taken priority and Tobias' uncle didn't watch it much now anyway.

Moving across the room and to the kitchen, Tobias pulled a bowl out from a cupboard and filled it with Scavenger's favourite meal of cat food and cornflakes. He watched as his friend devoured it like it was his first meal in months. Occasionally Scavenger would come up from his bowl just long enough to lick the orange cornflake dust from his nose before ploughing straight back in.

'Toby,' Tobias' uncle yelled from another room.

Tobias flinched at the sound, but the response was an instinctive one, developed from years of abuse. It was not a reaction which was even needed anymore.

In the four months since Tobias had returned, his uncle had not touched a drop of alcohol, and for the most part, his temper had been held in check. There had been hard times of course. Times when his uncle would demand a drink and couple the demand with threats of violence. But Tobias was also different now. Such threats no longer scared him like they used to. He had weathered such times with patience and resilience, staring his uncle down when needed, and comforting him as much as he was able.

Now, when his uncle yelled, it was not out of anger or malice but the desperate pleading of a man struggling with withdrawal.

'Toby,' his uncle called again, his voice weak and croaky.

'I'm coming,' Tobias shouted back. He picked up a tray from the kitchen worktop. The food in the apartment was no longer microwave meals and mouldy leftovers. Instead Tobias had cupboards full of groceries to work with. Mary, a lady from down the hall, brought them each week. Occasionally she even spent some time sitting and chatting with his uncle. Tobias tried to stay out of the way while she was there but he was glad that his uncle had a friend.

This time Tobias made his uncle a hot bowl of porridge and honey with a banana on the side and a large glass of water to wash it all down. Taking the tray, he made his way to his uncle's room.

The man who greeted Tobias was not the hideous visage of torment that he had once been. He remained gaunt and pale, and his gray hair was still thinning on top of his head, but his eyes no longer looked eternally bloodshot and his skin had lost its sweaty sheen. He smelt better too. Especially since he had started bathing, and cleaning the few teeth he had left.

His time as a heavy drinker had taken its toll, but instead of monstrous, he now looked old. Old and weak.

Tobias carried the tray over and his uncle grunted with effort as he sat himself up in his bed so the tray could be placed on his lap.

'Thanks Toby,' he said. 'You're a good kid.'

'Do you need anything else?'

'Don't go worrying about me Toby. You have to get everything ready. Tomorrow is a big day.'

'Do I have to go?'

'It will be good for you,' his uncle replied as he tried lifting his water to his lips with trembling hands. 'Besides, it's because of me that you have been away from school this long, and I don't want you missing any more than you already have.'

'I could stay in case you need me.' Tobias reached out and steadied the glass while his uncle took a sip and set the drink back down on the tray.

'Don't worry. I've got Scavenger to keep me company, and Mondays are when Mary brings the shopping so I won't be alone.'

'But you might need help with the oven, or you might hurt yourself, or…'

'Now, now,' his uncle said, gently cutting him off. 'You know the deal. I get sober and you try to have a normal life. That's what you wanted.'

'I know but…I'm scared.'

'Scared? You have been through far worse than school, both with me, and that other place. You shouldn't be scared.'

Tobias had eventually told his uncle some of what had happened to him in the Underlands and to his surprise, his uncle had believed him. Of course it helped that Tobias had brought back proof, and that he left out many of the details. Still, he hadn't expected his uncle to so readily accept what he was told.

They didn't speak about it much, and for that Tobias was grateful. But now and again, his uncle would use it to try to encourage him. Now was one of those times.

'I should never have taken you out of school in the first place,' his uncle continued, now poking at his porridge with his spoon. 'That was my mistake. One of the many I am trying to make up for. The first step is getting you back so you don't grow up to be like me.'

'I would never end up like you.' The words were out of Tobias' mouth before he could stop himself. They were hard and cutting. He instantly regretted saying them, despite still feeling like his uncle deserved to hear it.

In response, his uncle's face fell into an even glummer expression than usual. He looked down at his meal to avoid meeting his nephew's eyes. 'I deserved that. You still need to go to school though.'

'I know.' Tobias slumped down onto the stool at the side of his uncle's bed.

'You know, you are a lot like your mum.'

Tobias looked up at his uncle with surprise. He had never spoken of Tobias' parents before. 'My mum?'

'Yeah. She was always worrying about stuff.' Tobias' uncle didn't look up from his porridge, but he didn't take a mouthful either. The spoon just hovered over the bowl, shaking slightly.

'I remember when your dad first introduced her to the family,' his uncle continued. 'She was so worried about making a good impression that she got herself all worked up. In the end, she was so tense that she actually bent one of your gran's good forks just by gripping it too hard.'

A short raspy laugh followed the words and Tobias was sure that he could see a tear form in the corner of his uncle's eye. He was about to ask more, but before he could, his uncle coughed loudly, clattered his spoon into the porridge bowl, and quickly changed the subject.

'Anyway,' he said. 'Enough about the past. We need to think about your future. Now go and get your things together.'

As Tobias left his uncle's room, he could hear the grunts of pain as the man twisted himself around and tried to get more comfortable. Scavenger was listening too and was sitting just outside the doorway with a tilted head and sad looking eyes.

'He will be okay,' Tobias reassured both Scavenger and himself. 'He is still very poorly but he's getting better.'

Chapter 3

The following day came around much faster than Tobias would have liked. He had barely slept all night, and while that had mercifully kept the nightmares at bay, it had resulted in him spending the time thinking about school.

He couldn't remember the last time he had been around so many people, let alone have to speak to them. The idea of having to be in a completely alien environment while going to classes and making friends, was intimidating to say the least. That morning, as he had stared up at his ceiling, clutching his parents photo tight to his chest, he had found himself thinking that the prospect of school was even more terrifying than once again facing the Underlands.

It was a ridiculous thought and he knew it, but when he found himself staring up at the massive white building later that same day, the idea crept into his mind once again.

Two concrete paths cut through a neatly cut grass field and ran towards the building. While the one leading to the front reception was relatively quiet, the other was barely visible beneath a bustling torrent of children and teachers all heading in for the start of the school day.

Tobias couldn't help but think that they looked like an army of ants, all marching in chaotic formation but with unified purpose towards the same destination. They disappeared from sight into the rear playground.

Taking one last deep calming breath, Tobias hurried along the path which led to the automatic doors of the school reception. It took a moment for them to slide open, but once they did, he stepped through and approached the desk.

The woman sitting on the other side of the glass screen was a white haired old lady, peering through narrow spectacles at her computer screen and tapping away at the keyboard with a slow but regular rhythm. Tobias waited, shifting nervously and hoping that she would, at some point, look up and notice him. When she didn't, he gave a small cough.

'Oh, hello there,' she said, finally looking up from her work. 'Can I help you?'

'Erm, yeah. It's my first day,' Tobias replied weakly.

'Oh how exciting. What's your name sweety?'

'Tobias Crow.'

The woman pushed her spectacles further up the bridge of her nose and resumed typing on her computer. 'Ah yes. Here we are,' she said with one last click of a key. 'Come with me.'

Dropping her glasses so they hung from a cord around her neck, the woman lifted herself out of her chair and moved around to the large double doors which led further into the school. Pulling them open, she let Tobias through, and guided him along a narrow corridor.

Tobias followed close behind, shuffling his feet and glancing through every open door they passed as if he was expecting something to jump out at him at any moment. There were a handful of small offices, a kitchen, and what looked like a storeroom, but nothing really scary or out of place.

'Feeling a little nervous are we?' The receptionist asked as Tobias glanced into yet another small office.

'Just a bit,' Tobias replied, trying to look a little bit more confident than he actually felt.

'Let me guess.' The woman stopped and looked down at Tobias with a warm smile. 'You're feeling a tad worried about making friends?'

'I guess. I haven't been to school in ages.'

'Home schooled were you?'

'Something like that.'

'Well, there's no need to worry here, sweety. We are a welcoming little school. You will be making plenty of friends in no time. And if anyone does go and give you problems, you just tell them Mrs. Quint will come and sort them out. I'll show them what for.'

'Thanks.' Tobias gave her a genuine smile and she patted him on the shoulder. Despite her words, Tobias doubted anyone could be scared of such a sweet old woman.

'Now come on. Can't keep the head waiting.'

Reaching the end of the corridor, Mrs. Quint approached a closed door and knocked gently.

'Yes?' came a voice from the other side.

'Tobias Crow to see you Mr Fenwick.'

'Ah, excellent. Please let him in.'

The office on the other side of the door looked like it had once been a spacious room, but was now cluttered and cramped with very little space to move. A large window dominated one wall while bookcases and shelves filled the others. Ornaments and knicknacks battled for space amongst a mixed collection of shiny new textbooks and dusty old classics, while sticky notes and papers stuck out in seemingly random places.

In the centre of the room sat a huge wooden desk which, while plain, had clearly been designed for a much larger space. Behind this desk a tall, leather office chair strained under the weight of a portly man who Tobias assumed was Mr. Fenwick.

He looked like he was in his late forties with a round belly, bald head and a large, bushy, brown moustache. Leaning over the desk, he shook Tobias' hand and smiled at him with a wide grin which made his puffy cheeks rise so high that his eyes narrowed.

'Hello there Tobias,' Mr. Fenwick said as he leaned back in his seat. 'It is a pleasure to meet you.'

'You too sir,' Tobias replied quietly.

'Now, now Tobias. No need to be shy. We are all friends here and it is my job to make sure you settle in to school with no fuss and plenty of fun. Would you like a Jelly Baby?'

Mr Fenwick pulled a small glass bowl full of small jelly sweets out from a desk drawer and offered them to Tobias. Tobias just shook his head.

'You sure? They are awfully good.'

'No thank you sir.'

'Very well.' Mr Fenwick took a small handful for himself, popped one into his mouth and then dropped the bowl back into its drawer.

'Now then,' Mr Fenwick continued, still chewing around the sweet. 'I have the results of your entrance assessments here, and they are remarkably good for a child who has missed so much of his education. You are a very smart young man, Tobias.'

'Thank you sir.'

'I am certain that with a mind as sharp as yours, you will be catching up in no time.'

Mr. Fenwick paused for a moment and his round face took on a very serious expression. 'I am also aware of the difficult situation surrounding your guardianship, but I want you to know that I am here if you ever need any support or help. I want you to come to me if you have any problems. Any at all. Do you understand?'

'Yes sir,' Tobias replied and the man's face instantly broke back into a happy smile.

'Of course, there is nothing wrong with having a non-traditional family,' he said as another jelly sweet disappeared into his mouth. 'Nothing wrong with it at all. I myself have looked after several foster children so I am well accustomed to special circumstances.'

Tobias didn't reply. He doubted that the head teacher had encountered circumstances quite as *'special'* as his.

When Tobias didn't speak, Mr. Fenwick continued. 'I understand that your uncle has been very ill recently. Is he getting any better?'

'Yes sir. Much better.'

'Excellent. I want you to feel safe here Tobias. I know you have been through a lot with your home life, but you have help now. Please make as much use of it as you need.'

Tobias was feeling more and more uncomfortable with the way the conversation was going and he just wanted it to be over. He had heard so many adults offering him support since his uncle had agreed to get help, but he knew none of them could truly help him. None of them knew what he had really been through, or what problems he still faced. It wasn't even as if he could tell them. No one would believe him.

'Yes sir,' was all he said in reply.

Obviously realising that the conversation wasn't going to go any further, Mr Fenwick lifted himself unsteadily to his feet and threw the last of the sweets into his mouth. They joined the one he was already chewing and it took him a moment before he had swallowed enough to be able to speak again.

'Well then,' he said as he waddled for the door. 'I guess we better get you to your new class and make introductions. I'm putting you in Mr Buckle's tutor group.'

Mr Fenwick led Tobias out of the office and through the school, pointing out places of interest along the way.

'This is the main building,' he said cheerfully as they walked along a wide corridor lined with lockers and classrooms. 'Down there is where you will find the humanities and english rooms. Over there is the library. Oh, and over here is the main lunch hall. You will be provided with a meal card of course.'

Tobias was trying to listen but he was finding himself a little overwhelmed by the size of the place and it was hard to remember which way was which.

Finally they came to a classroom at the end of a short hallway and Mr Fenwick stepped inside. Tobias watched as he exchanged some quiet words with a tall, black haired teacher who Tobias assumed must be Mr. Buckle. The man looked half asleep as he slouched in his chair. His eyes hung half closed, his clothes were crumpled, and his face was coated in a short, grey flecked stubble.

Mr. Fenwick gestured wildly as he spoke and in response, Mr. Buckle just listened impassively, the only movement being a lazy nod right before Mr. Fenwick turned and beckoned for Tobias to enter.

'Good morning class,' said Mr Fenwick as he guided Tobias by the shoulders so that they were standing at the front of the classroom. It was an intimidating place to be, with the eyes of over twenty five other children all watching him. All of them would be wondering who he was and what he was doing there.

'Good morning,' all the children chimed out together. Still none of them seemed to tear their gaze off of the new boy. For his part, Mr Fenwick seemed blissfully unaware of Tobias' discomfort as he continued to address the class.

'I hope your weekends were all fun filled and eventful, and that you are all bright eyed and bushy tailed, ready to get back to some good hard work.'

In reply all the children groaned in unison with a vague 'yes' noise.

'Excellent. Now, I have some very exciting news. This young man here is Tobias Crow and he will be joining your class on your epic adventures of education and enlightenment.'

Tobias looked out at the faces glaring back at him. He knew it was probably his imagination but it felt like every single one of them was staring with malicious intent, judging him and silently hating him.

'Now Tobias is completely new to the school,' Mr Fenwick continued, 'so I need a very special volunteer to take him under their wing and make sure we make him feel as welcome as possible.'

Suddenly, every one of the children in the room broke eye contact with Tobias as they all found something else to look at. Some stared out the window, some down at their table and others looked up at the ceiling. All of them were desperately trying not to draw attention to themselves. All of them except one.

A girl in the front row was waving her arm around as if she was trying to get the attention of someone a hundred miles away, despite it actually being less than a couple of metres. She was a thin-limbed, almost gangly girl with long blond hair, a face full of freckles and a pair of large, round rimmed glasses perched precariously on her nose.

'Miss Liddle,' Mr Fenwick greeted her with a beaming smile. 'I knew I could count on you.'

'Thank you sir,' the girl replied with a proud nod of the head.

Apparently happy that his job was done, Mr Fenwick turned back to Tobias. 'Well there we are Tobias. Miss Liddle will help you get settled and if you need anything at all, my door is always open.' With that he turned on his heels and wobbled out of the room.

As the door swung closed all the faces were suddenly back, looking straight at Tobias but this time murmurs and whispers filled the air.

'That's enough. You all know what you should be doing,' said Mr Buckle who was still lounging in his chair. Looking at Tobias he added, 'Bell will be going in five minutes and then you will be in History. Here is your timetable. Now get a seat and wait quietly. Good lad.'

Chapter 4

As soon as the bell rang, signalling that morning registration had ended, everyone began spilling out from the room. Mr Buckle barely looked up from a book he was reading as he mumbled, 'see you all after dinner.'

Tobias remained in his seat for as long as possible and watched as the majority of the other children bumped and barged their way through the door. Once the initial rush had abated, he grabbed his bag and stepped nervously out into the corridor. That was when the freckled girl rushed over like an excited puppy. She was practically bouncing as she caught up to him and landed right in his path with a cheerful bound.

'Hi there,' she said.

'Erm... Hi.'

'Tobias isn't it? Well it's a pleasure to meet you. My name is Kayt, K-A-Y-T, Kayt. It's an odd spelling I know but my dad says it's better to be unusual than boring and I guess he is right. Anyway, you're new aren't you? Have you just moved? Do you live close to the school? I just live with my Dad. Do you live with your parents? What about pets? Do you have pets? You look like you would have pets?'

All the words tumbled out of her mouth like a tidal wave and Tobias struggled to keep up with what she was saying. Even her body seemed to be buzzing with a nervous energy which meant she couldn't seem to stand still. Before Tobias could even get his bearings or process what she had said, she was suddenly silent and staring at him expectantly.

'Sorry,' he replied after a long pause. 'I didn't catch all that.'

'Oh yeah, sorry about that. People say I talk too much but I don't really notice it. Do you? Notice it I mean. Not talk too much. I just say what I am thinking. Which I suppose could come across as talking too much, but it doesn't hurt to be friendly does it. Do you have many friends yet? We could be friends if you want. Do you want to be friends?'

Tobias smiled. 'Sure.'

In a weird sort of way Kayt reminded him of Scavenger, and she seemed like she did genuinely just want to be friends.

To his surprise Kayt squealed with glee and jumped at him, wrapping her arms around his body and squeezing tight in a hug which forced all the air from his lungs. Her glasses pushed against his shoulder and frizzy strands of her hair stuck to his face.

'Oh wow,' she said when she let go. 'This is awesome. I don't have many friends, but I just know we will be best buddies in no time. It will be great. So, what do you like to do? You know, hobbies and the like?'

Before Tobias could answer another bell rang out through the school and Kayt began skipping off down the hall. 'Come on,' she shouted back to him. 'That bell means we are already late. It's history next. I love history. We are learning about Cleopatra. You can sit next to me.'

'Well she is a crazy one,' Tobias whispered to himself as Kayt rounded a corner and disappeared from sight. Then, realising that he was alone and had no idea where he was meant to be going, he darted after her.

The rest of the day was far more fun than Tobias had ever imagined. He spent the whole day being shown around by Kayt. Her strange, wild energy was contagious and he felt like he had laughed more in those few hours than he had in the rest of his life put together.

They went to history class, maths, english and geography. They even sat together at dinner, and though Tobias barely got a word out, he was glad for such cheerful company. He was more than happy to sit and listen as Kayt reeled off her entire family history, as well as her hobbies, musical tastes and favourite foods.

'Have you ever read Lovecraft?' Kayt asked as they walked out of the main doors at the end of the school day?

'I don't really read a lot.' Tobias replied.

'Oh you should. He is great. Well, his stories are great. I don't actually know him. Not personally anyway. I'll bring one of my books tomorrow for you to read.'

'That would be great. Thanks.'

'No problem bestie.' Kayt punched him gently on the shoulder and they both laughed.

They walked a little further along the road and the crowds of other school children began to thin and fade as groups split off to walk their own ways home. Eventually it was just Tobias and Kayt walking alone towards the corner where Tobias would need to part ways. That was when Kayt came to a dead stop and her voice went uncharacteristically silent.

'What is it?' Tobias asked.

'It's Jay.'

'Jay?'

'Jay Adler. Over there.'

Kayt pointed along the road, past the corner and to the street ahead. Sat, lounging on a low wall was a boy. He looked a little bit older than Tobias and Kayt, probably fourteen or fifteen, and he was big. His shoulders were broad, his neck almost as thick as his head, and his hair was cut so short it was barely there. His square face, which was dominated by a broad flat nose, made Tobias think of a bull.

'Who is he?'

'He's a big dumb meathead and a bully who is always hanging outside his house when I walk past. I'm sure he only does it so he can pick on me. Dad says he is probably lonely, or insecure, or something, which is why he lashes out. I think he's just mean though.'

'Do you want to go a different way?'

'There isn't one. My street runs off his. It's okay though. You can go. I can handle him.'

Tobias thought about leaving, heading home and staying away from danger. It's what he would have done before.

'I'll walk with you,' he said instead, and grabbing Kayt's wrist he pulled her onwards. 'Come on. I'm right next to you.'

As the pair got closer to Jay's house, the boy looked up and locked eyes with them. His flat face split in a nasty looking grin.

'Hey freako!' he shouted as he hopped down off the wall and planted himself firmly in the middle of the path. 'Who's your friend?'

'Leave us alone Jay,' Kayt replied. She sounded defiant but her head was held low, her shoulders slumped and she kept fiddling with her glasses, pushing them further up her freckled nose. It was body language that Tobias was familiar with. He had felt the same sense of intense discomfort himself many times.

'Leave you alone?' Jay laughed. It was deep and loud. 'Why? I just want to say hello to your little friend freako.'

Jay stepped up in front of them and blocked their way. He towered over Tobias and puffed out his barrel chest so that he appeared even larger. Tobias tried not to show any fear, but the boy seemed giant compared to him and he couldn't help but notice how thickly muscled Jay's arms were.

'Who is he then?' Jay asked, stepping even closer and forcing Tobias to move backwards. 'Is he your boyfriend freako?'

'Stop calling her that!' Tobias tried to sound confident. He felt stupid allowing a petty bully to intimidate him when he had battled with the Witch Mother.

'Why should I? What are you going to do wimp?'

'I… I…' Tobias tried to think of something defiant to say but his mind was completely blank and his stuttering efforts only seemed to make Jay even more confident.

'Pathetic,' he laughed and he shoved Tobias hard in the chest, sending him sprawling to the floor.

'Oi!' Kayt yelled as she jumped in between them and held her arms out wide. 'Leave him alone.'

Tobias was only dimly aware of her voice. Another voice had caught his attention. A sinister and angry voice that emanated deep at the back of his own mind.

'Punish him,' it purred darkly. 'Make him suffer. Make him weep. You have the power. You have control. You can destroy him.'

'Shut up,' he hissed under his breath but he could feel the anger building and the darkness deep within his soul straining to escape.

'Come on freako,' he heard Jay say as the boy grabbed Kayt by the wrist and pulled her away from Tobias. 'Leave the wimp there.'

Tobias looked up at Kayt. Tears were forming in her eyes and she was rubbing them away with the back of her free hand. The glowing orange energy of fear was beginning to form around her. Tobias could not only see it but also feel it calling to him. The sensation was intoxicating, lulling him in and begging him to reach out and use his power. He pushed the feeling back into the deepest part of his mind. This was not him. It was Tyringar and he could not allow it to take control.

'Get off her!' he shouted as he got to his feet. He ignored the intense desire to manifest the fear and to seriously hurt Jay. Instead he clenched his fist and drove it forward as hard as he could. It connected with the boy's back, but it felt like punching a solid wall.

Jay grunted as the blow connected. Much to Tobias' surprise, he even let go of Kayt's arm. The victory was short-lived however. Jay spun on the spot, striking him hard in the face and sending him to the ground once more. Tobias spun as he fell and both his knees, and the palms of his hands, scraped against the concrete as he landed. His face throbbed where Jay's fist had connected. It was a familiar sensation but one that he had not felt since his uncle had stopped drinking.

'Pathetic,' Jay said before turning away and stalking off down his driveway. 'Catch you later freako.'

As soon as the boy disappeared into his house, Kayt was straight over by Tobias' side, helping him to his feet. 'Are you okay?'

'I'm fine,' Tobias replied.

'I'm sorry about him. He really is such a prat.'

'Seriously, It's fine. Are you okay?'

'Oh, I'm okay. Jay never really hurts me. He has pushed me around before, but mainly he just calls me names and won't leave me alone. Dad says he is probably unhappy, but I can't see how he can expect anything else when he acts so horrible. Are you sure you are okay? Your eye looks very red. It might bruise. Dad says you should put frozen peas on a bruise so it doesn't get too bad. I don't know if you have frozen peas, but if you do, it might be good to give it a try.'

'I will, thanks.' Tobias smiled and Kayt smiled back at him.

'Okay. I guess I best let you get home but is it okay if we hang out tomorrow?'

'I would like that.'

'Awesome.'

Kayt jumped forward and wrapped her arms around Tobias in a massive hug, before running off down the road shouting 'See you tomorrow,' as she did.

Despite his grazes, Tobias walked the rest of the way home in high spirits. He had spent most of his life being the victim of violence, but that didn't mean that he had to give into the fear like he used to. He had helped a friend, and more importantly, he had resisted the dark desires of Tyringar. Both of which he counted as a worthwhile victory.

Chapter 5

The next four days of school were a very mixed experience for Tobias. He enjoyed spending time with Kayt. She always seemed genuinely pleased to see him, and their time together was always full of smiles, laughter, and fun.

Unfortunately, few of the other children at the school were as welcoming as Kayt. In fact, as the week progressed, Tobias felt more and more like an oddity. One which his fellow students were only willing to observe from a distance and never approach.

'You need to make the first move,' his uncle had told him. 'Approach them and start a conversation. Once they get to know you, they will be begging to be your friends.'

So, on Thursday morning, after three days of Kayt being his only friend, Tobias decided to follow his uncle's advice. He waited until after the morning registration, when Mr. Buckle had absently dismissed the class, and approached a group of his fellow students. He knew their names and from overhearing some of their conversations, he also knew that they liked football. His uncle used to watch football a lot and Tobias was confident that he had learned enough about the sport to have a conversation.

Taking a deep breath and summoning up as much courage as he could manage, Tobias approached the boys.

'Hi,' he said, stepping in behind a dark haired boy named Ryan.

Ryan replied with a half hearted smile and an offhand 'hi,' before turning back to his friends.

'Who's up for a game at lunch?' A boy named Tyler asked the rest of the group. They all gave an eager mutter of agreement.

Despite feeling like he was being openly ignored, Tobias persevered. 'Are you playing football?' He asked.

'Yeah,' Ryan replied without even turning around.

'Can I play?'

There was a long pause as everyone in the group shot each other awkward looks. Eventually Ryan shook his head and turned to face Tobias without actually making eye contact.

'I don't think so.'

'Yeah,' Tyler added. 'We already have enough players '

'It's okay,' Tobias lied. 'I get it.'

'Sorry, mate,' Ryan said before he and the other boys wandered off down the corridor to their first class.

Tobias watched them go. They were already chatting and laughing normally by the time they rounded the corner. Tobias felt his shoulders sag slightly and his head dropped to his chest.

'You okay?' Kayt asked.

'I just don't get it,' Tobias replied. 'Why won't they even give me a chance?'

'They are all Jerks,' Kayt replied. 'Big stinky jerks. They have made their friends and don't like letting anyone else in. Especially people like us.'

'People like us?'

'You know, people who are different. My dad always says that it is good to be different, but I'm not so sure. I don't think people like it when someone is different because they are all busy pretending that they are normal even if they aren't. That's why I don't really have many friends. They all think I'm odd.'

'Do you think I'm odd?' Tobias asked. He didn't think he was odd. After everything he had been through, he knew he was definitely different, but the other children didn't know that. He thought he had been acting completely normal.

Kayt thought a moment before replying. 'I wouldn't say you were odd exactly. Not that there would be anything wrong with it if you were. I think everyone just sees you as different because you are new. They don't know you, and people can be scared of what they don't know.'

There was a momentary pause before, in an unhappy tone, Kayt added, 'It probably doesn't help that you are hanging around with me. I'm not exactly popular.'

Tobias looked up at his friend. She was purposely avoiding eye contact by staring down at the floor and her usual beaming face had fallen into a look of sadness.

Tobias gave her a friendly punch to the shoulder before saying, 'I don't care what they think. I like you and I'm glad we are friends.'

'Really?'

'Yeah. I like odd.'

Kayt's smile slowly began to break back through and she looked up. 'We can be odd together.'

'Sounds good to me.'

'Good, because I love being your friend. And I'm not just saying that because you are the only real friend I have. I would be your friend even if I was the most popular girl in school.

Although, I suppose if I was the most popular girl in school, and you were my friend, you would probably be popular too, so this wouldn't really be a problem. But you know what I mean.'

'I think so,' Tobias said with a chuckle.

Maybe Kayt really was the only friend he needed. It wasn't like he'd started with a lot of friends, so one extra was still way more than he had before.

The two of them continued in silence until they rounded the final corner and the dining hall came into view. Unfortunately, standing in between them and their destination was the hulking form of Jay Adler, flanked by two other boys. They weren't as large as Jay but they looked the same age and just as mean.

'I've been asking around about you, wimp,' Jay said.

'Let's go another way,' Kayt said, but before they had a chance to change direction, the three boys circled them, with Jay taking up position right at the front.

He leaned down so he was looking straight into Kayt's face.

'Do you know why wimp hasn't been in school before?' He asked. 'It's because he lives with a crazy uncle who kept him locked up. It was in a tower block too.'

Jay laughed loudly at the last statement and his companions sniggered along with him.

'Locked up in a tower,' Jay continued. 'He is like a fairytale princess. Are you a princess, wimp?'

'Don't talk about my uncle,' Tobias said. He meant for the words to be forceful and stern, but his fear was rising just as quickly as his anger, and it came out far quieter than he had intended.

'What was that? Don't talk about your crazy uncle? Why, what are you going to do about it?'

'Please leave it Jay,' Kayt begged but Jay was focused completely on Tobias. All her words earned her was more laughter from the other two boys.

'Come on, wimp. What are you going to do?'

Tobias dragged his eyes away from the floor and tried to look at the bully. Being scared of someone like Jay was ridiculous, but it was more than that. What if Jay was right? What if Tobias just didn't fit in? What if he never did?'

'Jay!' Kayt yelled. She stamped her foot for good measure.

'What? I can't help it if he is such a princess that he can't stand up for himself.'

'I can stand up for myself,' Tobias muttered darkly. If he was never going to fit in, then why pretend? Why not just let the darkness out?

Jay's laughter faltered when Tobias raised his gaze and stared straight at him. There was a definite flash of fear across the bullies face, but it was swiftly replaced by stubborn anger.

Tobias began feeling for the fear. Reaching out with his mind to twist into a tool for his fury. Then a hand clutched his shoulder.

'They aren't worth it,' Kayt said as she pulled him back.

All his fury melted in an instant. Kayt was his friend. She liked him, and it really didn't matter what someone like Jay thought. Or the rest of the children at the school. If they didn't like him just because he was new or different, that was their problem, not his.

Tobias allowed Kayt to guide him by the shoulder and turned away from Jay.

'Oi!' the bully shouted. Grabbing Tobias' other shoulder he tried to turn him back but was stopped by the arrival of a new voice.

'Excuse me gentlemen,' interrupted Mr. Fenwick, waddling up behind them.

'I do hope we aren't having any problems here,' the headmaster said with a pointed look in Jay's direction.

'Not at all sir,' Jay replied. 'We were just making Tobias feel welcome.'

Mr. Fenwick regarded the situation with a look of deep suspicion before finally nodding his head with a broad smile and saying 'Jolly good. Now hurry along or you will miss dinner.'

'Yes sir,' Jay and his friends said in unison before rushing off down the corridor.

Mr. Fenwick watched the boys disappear before turning back to Tobias. 'Young Mr. Adler wasn't giving you too much trouble was he?'

'Not really sir,' Tobias replied honestly. 'Nothing I can't handle.'

'Well, don't hesitate to come to me if you do have any problems.'

'Thank you sir, but I am fine.'

'I'm taking good care of him sir,' Kayt added and Mr. Fenwick gave them both an energetic nod.

'I am glad to hear it, Miss Liddle. Everyone needs a good friend.'

Chapter 6

'Are you serious?' Hex asked excitedly. Tobias had not only retrieved the stone from the back of the cupboard, but was currently looping its leather cord around his neck.

'Yeah,' Tobias replied. 'It's the weekend and I thought you could do with getting out of the flat.'

'Not that I am complaining, but why the sudden change of heart?'

Tobias looked down at the twisting purple mist that was Hex's trapped soul. 'I don't know. I guess I just don't feel as angry as I did before.'

'I must admit, you do seem to be in fine spirits.'

'I feel great.' Tobias replied. 'In fact, I feel better than great. I feel awesome. School is going well, my uncle is getting better and I've actually been having fun.'

'Well I am glad to hear it, and I am extremely grateful to be getting out of this flat for a bit, but please don't get too complacent. You still have to be on guard, remember.'

'Do you really think the Witch Mother will still be after me?'

'She will never stop. You are a threat to her and as soon as she can find a way to reach you, she will be coming.'

'So what should I do? Just sit in my room and hide for the rest of my life?' Tobias tucked Hex beneath his t-shirt and pulled on his jacket.

'Of course not. All I'm saying is you need to be ready. Do not get too comfortable.'

'Don't have fun you mean.'

'That's not what I am saying. Just stay on guard. That's all.'

'Fine, I'll stay on guard, but at some point, I want to have a normal life.'

'I know, I know,' Hex said with a sigh. 'Look, just forget I said anything. Enjoy your day and we can talk about it later.'

Tobias nodded and grabbed his bag before heading for the front door.

'I'm going out,' he called to his uncle.

'Be safe,' his uncle called back.

'I will.'

Letting the door swing shut behind him, Tobias ran for the stairs, leaping down the last couple on each floor and going faster and faster as he did.

Kayt was waiting for him on their usual corner. The same spot where they would meet everyday to walk to school and where they would say goodbye after school had finished.

When Kayt saw Tobias approaching, she didn't even try to control her excitement and instantly began jumping up and down, waving her hand so frantically that her glasses wobbled on her nose and she had to stop to correct them before they fell off.

'Hey Tobias, over here,' she called over to him.

'Hi Kayt,' he called back before picking up his pace and closing the gap between them. 'Thanks for agreeing to meet up. It's nice to get out and do something that isn't school.'

'Don't mention it. I'm happy to meet up anytime. No one has ever asked me to meet up outside school before. Of course, no one has ever asked to meet up inside school before either, but dad said I have to make more of an effort to make friends, so here I am. I told him all about you by the way. He said you seem nice. From what I've told him anyway.'

Tobias smiled as they began walking side by side. He really liked being around Kayt. She was so happy and energetic, it was easy to forget everything else that had happened to him. He also liked the fact that she talked so much. It meant that he didn't have to. The last thing he wanted to do, at any time, was talk about himself.

'So what do you want to do?' Kayt asked. 'We could go to the park. It's got a little wooded patch with walks and trails and stuff, and I know loads of little hiding spots. I say hiding spots but the woods aren't huge. Still, if you go off the path, the bushes are thick enough that no one can see you, so it's kind of like having hiding spots. Me and my dad made a den there once. It didn't last long but it was pretty cool.'

'The park sounds good.'

'Awesome. Lets go.'

Kayt shot off down the street at full sprint and Tobias was momentarily caught off guard by the sudden movement.

'Hey, wait up,' he called after her. Pulling his backpack straps tighter so that the bag didn't bounce around too much, he chased after her.

Although Kayt slowed following her initial rush, it still only took ten minutes for them to reach the low metal railings which marked the boundary of the park. Kayt hopped up and over the fence, stumbling slightly as she landed on the other side. She would have fallen over completely if she hadn't grabbed a railing to balance herself at the last minute.

'Probably should have just used the gate,' She said as she looked back at Tobias with a slightly embarrassed grin.

'Probably,' Tobias laughed in reply as he swung himself over and landed with a bit more care than she had. He was careful to keep his backpack steady so that he didn't drop it.

Once they were both safely on the other side, Kayt pushed her glasses back up her nose and rushed off once again towards the treeline which was on the other side of a large football pitch and a brightly painted play area with swings, a slide and a climbing frame.

The woods were not exactly what Tobias had been expecting. When Kayt had first mentioned them, his mind had automatically thought back to the vast green land of Terrascura, which he had trekked through when escaping the Underlands.

This patch of trees, however, was about as far from that lush jungle-like world as they could possibly be. It was little more than a cluster of crooked trunks and spindly branches, bulked out by tall weeds and fat thorny bushes covered in small green leaves. Despite this, Tobias could see that Kayt was excited to show him her hiding spots so he dutifully followed as she plunged into a small gap between two bushes and pushed her way through to a small space within.

'Here we are,' she said as she held her arms out to show off the area. It was a domed cave of leaves and branches with a patch of clear earth in the centre. An opening in the top allowed sunlight to peer in, and the few branches which had grown inwards had been bent back on themselves and woven into the wall of the structure.

Tobias looked around and he had to admit, although the bushes were far from the thick foliage he had expected, they were indeed thick enough that you couldn't see out and no one would be able to see in.

'What do you think?'

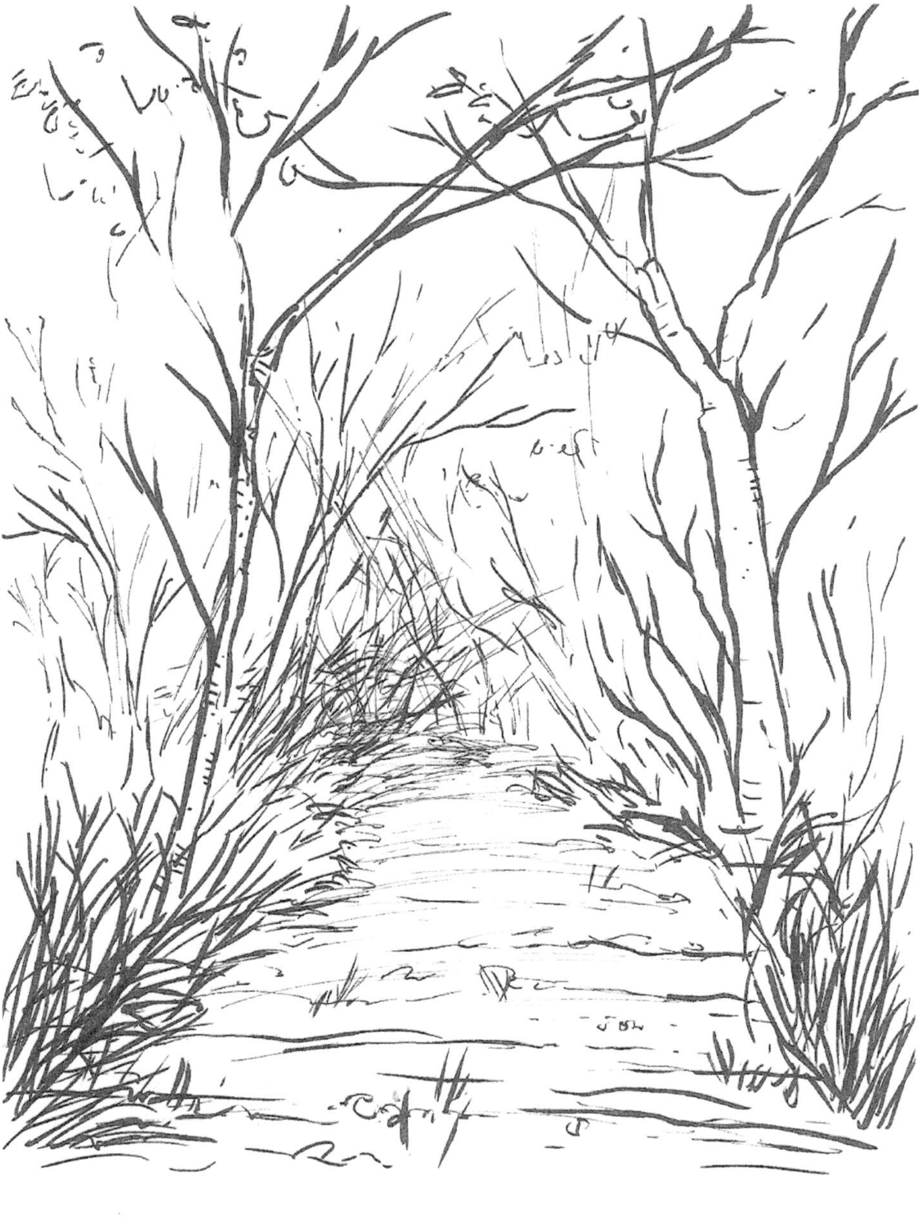

'I like it,' Tobias replied as he pulled his backpack off and sat himself down on the hard packed dirt.

'Thanks. This is one of my favourite hiding spots because no one knows I'm here. It's great when Jay is in the park or when I just want to read in peace. How about you? Do you like hiding?'

'I used to. I would hide a lot, but I don't do it much anymore.'

'What happened?'

'I guess I just realised that it didn't help much. I am braver now than I used to be.'

'That's cool.'

Tobias looked at Kayt for a moment. He was pretty sure he could trust her. 'Can you keep a secret?'

'Of course,' she replied immediately as she sat herself down opposite him. 'I keep secrets all the time. Mostly my own of course, but that still counts doesn't it? Either way, you can trust me, I don't tell anyone anything that I shouldn't. My Dad says I am the biggest chatter mouth he has ever met, but I would never tell a secret.'

'Okay, okay,' Tobias laughed. 'I want you to meet someone.'

With that he pulled his backpack into his lap and slowly unzipped the top. Kayt leaned in closer, her curiosity clearly getting the better of her. When the zip was open, Tobias reached in and began moving aside the blanket he had put in as padding.

Once he had made a big enough gap, Scavenger's chubby, flat nosed face sprung up out of the bag with a happy squeak. The creature's ears took a moment to fully unfurl but once they did, he pricked them up and stared straight at Kayt. Her face was a mix of total shock and startled wonder but Scavenger examined her like she was the oddity.

'W-what is it?'

'His name is Scavenger. He is my friend.'

'Is he like a dog or a mouse or something?'

'Erm, I would say he is definitely a something.'

As Tobias replied, Kayt slowly reached out a hand and moved it very carefully towards Scavenger's head. It was like she was expecting him to jump up and bite her at any minute. When he didn't, and her hand eventually reached his head, she began stroking him gingerly. Scavenger responded by pushing his head upwards into her palm and rubbing it backwards and forwards against her skin.

Kayt giggled. 'He is awesome.'

'I thought you would like him,' Tobias replied. 'I wanted to bring him so he could get some exercise. He doesn't get out much.'

Tobias pulled more of the blanket aside so that the full, round, form of Scavenger was visible. No longer trapped by the soft woolen bonds, Scavenger eagerly jumped out the bag and landed on the ground beside it. He then spent several seconds stretching and loosening himself up. He shook out his thick back legs and allowed his tail to unfurl behind him before hopping around in a small circle to examine his new surroundings.

Kayt watched it all in amazed fascination. She even seemed lost for words for the first time since Tobias had met her. 'Seriously, what is it?'

'I actually don't know. I just, kind of, found him. Well, I guess he found me really.'

'Well he is awesome.'

Chapter 7

The late afternoon sun was already setting when Tobias and Kayt decided to call it a day. The sun had long past its peak and it was dipping down towards the horizon, producing a soft orange glow which cast long shadows across the ground.

The two children had talked and laughed for hours, not really discussing anything. Just enjoying each other's company. Even Scavenger had delighted in being outdoors, rushing in and out of bushes, munching on leaves, and bouncing around Kayt as she laughed hysterically and used a long blade of grass to try and tickle him whenever he came close.

Tobias could have happily stayed even later but both their stomachs were starting to rumble and the day was getting late.

'Dad will wonder where I've got to,' Kayt said. 'He will probably panic if I'm not home for tea. He says I should have a mobile phone so he can get hold of me, but I keep losing them. I think he has just given up now. It's pie for tea tonight.'

'I should really get back to my uncle too.' Tobias replied. I'm cooking burgers.'

'You do the cooking?'

Tobias realised that it probably wasn't normal for a boy his age to do the cooking. Let alone the cleaning, washing and laundry. He also realised that admitting such things would likely result in some awkward and uncomfortable questions which he really didn't want to answer. So in the end he just replied with, 'Yeah, sometimes.'

'That's cool. I doubt my dad would trust me with the cooking. He lets me make toast and stuff but not use the oven or anything. I do the dishes sometimes though. It's not much fun, but I guess it's a lot harder to burn the house down with a tub of soapy water than it is with an oven.'

'I'm sure if anyone could do it, it would be you,' Tobias said with a laugh.

Kayt gave him a playful punch to the arm before admitting, 'You are probably right.'

'Anyway,' she added. 'We really should get going. Can we do this again though?'

'Oh, definitely,' Tobias replied before calling Scavenger back and gently tucking the chubby rodent back into his bag. Kayt gave the funny little creature one last pat before he snuggled in under his blanket.

'Will you bring him again next time too?' She asked as they climbed through the bushes and back into the park.

'Yeah sure. To be honest he needs the exercise.'

Tobias was about to say more but he stopped when he noticed that Kayt had halted in her tracks and was staring at the play area with a look of definite concern.

Tobias followed her gaze and quickly realised the problem. Leaning against the metal frame of the slide was the unmistakable bulk of Jay Adler. He was surrounded by five smaller kids who were staring up at him like he was a king. But despite having the full attention of his adoring fans, Jay had clearly seen the two of them emerge and his attention had shifted completely onto his new targets.

'Hey,' Jay called over, dismissing his little audience and breaking away from them to advance on Tobias and Kayt.

'Well, well,' he continued. 'If it isn't Freako and the wimp. What are you two doing in the bushes eh? Were you kissing?' He pulled his face into a mock look of disgust as he spoke. 'I don't know which is worse, him kissing you, or you kissing him.'

'Leave us alone Jay,' Kayt replied. She tried to walk past but he swung out a thick arm to block her way.

'I'm just having a bit of fun with you. Don't you want to have fun.'

Tobias stepped forward and met Jay's gaze. He could feel his anger rising and the voice in the back of his head beginning to murmur, but it was easy to ignore. All he wanted to do was get around this thuggish idiot and go home. Unfortunately, whatever it was he was going to say was lost when the screaming started.

The sound startled all three of them and it took Tobias a moment to realise that it was coming from Jay's group of friends, who until that point, had still been in the play area. Now every single one of them was darting frantically away from the slide and sprinting as fast as they could towards the park exit.

Turning his attention away from the frightened kids and back towards the play area, Tobias saw the source of their sudden terror.

Perched atop the slide, crouched low and staring straight in his direction was a huge, jet black, cat. It looked like a panther with a sleek body and a broad, flat face. But this was definitely no normal panther. For one thing, its legs were far too well muscled and bulged beneath the fur. Worse than that though was where a panther would only have two front legs, this thing had four.

Tobias instantly knew this beast was not from the mortal realm, and the thought of where it may well be from, sent a tremor of genuine terror shooting up his spine.

'What the hell is that?' Jay muttered as he too took in the sight.

'Run Tobias!' Hex's voice yelled out from beneath his clothes and even though it drew intensely confused looks from both Jay and Kayt, neither of them had a chance to react before Tobias had grabbed Kayt's hand and began sprinting for his life.

He heard a loud creak of metal followed by a crash, and then a thud as something landed on the ground behind him. It sounded much closer than he would have liked. Instinctively he began the mantra that he hadn't used since escaping the Underlands.

Don't look back, it only slows you down.

Don't think of the danger, panic makes you falter.

Don't run in a straight line, it makes you easier to catch.

Keep your head low and keep running till you can't run anymore. If you stop or slow, it will get you.

He also reached for his hip where he had once kept Fear Bane, the weapon that helped him focus his powers. Unfortunately, the weapon was not there. It hadn't been since he had returned to the mortal realm. It was tucked under his bed.

'You don't need it,' a voice whispered deep at the back of his mind. 'Let me out and I can save you all.'

Tobias ignored it and kept running.

There was another thud, this time even closer.

Kayt's grip on Tobias' hand tightened. 'Tobias?' she began but he didn't even acknowledge that she had spoken. This was not the time for talking. This was the time for running.

The fence was not far now. Just a short sprint and they would be through the gate and back into the street. It was still unclear what they would do once there, but Tobias had set this as his immediate goal and he was going to make it.

A final thud and the huge black beast landed right in their path, cutting them off completely and bringing them to a skidding halt. It was crouched low and rumbling with a menacing growl.

'No matter what happens, you have to run,' Tobias told Kayt. 'Run all the way home and do not stop until you get there.' He also shoved his backpack into her hands. Scavenger would be much safer with her.

'B-but,' Kayt began and Tobias swiftly cut her off.

'Don't argue, just run. It wants me, not you.'

Being honest with himself, Tobias didn't really know if this thing did want him, but he did know that it was the most likely reason it was there. He hoped that if he ran back into the park, it would follow him and leave Kayt alone. If he was lucky, he might just make the patch of trees before it caught him. He would have more of a chance amongst the low branches and knotted bushes.

Tobias let go of Kayt's hand and turned on his feet, ready to run back the way he had come, but before he could make his move, a new shape leapt in from the side.

A large shape that dived in head first and wrapped its arms tightly around the black cat's waist before taking it down to the ground in a flying tackle.

'Run Kayt!' Jay yelled as he wrestled with the beast, holding it as tight as he could with one arm while braying at its head with the other.

It was hard to say whether it was the sudden movement or the authority of the command which triggered a response, but whatever it was, Kayt did as she was told and immediately bolted for the park gate.

Tobias was about to follow but his legs didn't move. Jay had the creature but it wasn't a hold that he could maintain for long. Its rippling muscles were straining against his grip and one of its four front legs was clawing at his back, catching at his clothes and getting dangerously close to doing some real damage.

'What can I do?' Tobias asked, grabbing at the teardrop stone under his t-shirt.

'Run,' Hex replied without pause.

'No! How do I help Jay?'

'You can't. Just Run.'

Tobias cursed under his breath and looked around for something that he could use, but there was nothing.

'You have power,' the voice crooned in his head. 'You can have control. All you have to do is reach out and take it.'

'I can't,' Tobias replied out loud. 'I don't want to.'

'You have to. You can't save him unless you do.'

Tobias clenched his eyes tight and desperately tried to keep his mind focused, to hold onto the thoughts and will that were his own, while still allowing the power that festered deep within to creep to the surface.

'Yes,' the voice hissed in delight and smoky orange tendrils began forming around Tobias' now clenched fists. It wasn't much but he couldn't summon more without Fear Bane. Not without losing control completely.

Allowing the orange energy to solidify and take shape as two thin, razor sharp shards Tobias opened his eyes and extended his arms.

'Let Go!' he yelled out to Jay.

Jay was already losing his grip, and with one powerful flex of its muscles, the creature broke free. The surge of strength was too much for Jay and he was forced to release his hold and roll out of the way. As that happened, Tobias launched the shards.

They flew forward with incredible speed and sliced deep into the cat's thick, black flesh. One cut across its back above one of its left shoulders. The other gauged a deep cut from its left eye, causing its face to erupt in a shower of blood.

Neither blow was enough to drop the thing, but they definitely had an impact and it howled in pain before spinning around and bounding off across the park and disappearing over a tall brick wall that lined one edge of the football pitch.

Tobias watched it go and when he was certain it wasn't coming back, he collapsed to his knees. He felt drained and exhausted, like all the energy had been ripped from his body.

'Is it gone?' Kayt called out. 'Is everyone okay?' She hadn't run far but was instead huddled behind the entrance gatepost and was now peering around the corner with Scavenger wrapped in a tight cuddle at her chest.

'It's gone,' Tobias shouted weakly and then fell onto his back on the grass.

Chapter 8

Jay's eyes bore down on Tobias with an angry glare.

'What the hell was that?' The older boy demanded, as if he somehow knew that it was all Tobias' fault.

The other children had all scattered out of the park and had not returned, so with only the three of them left, Tobias, Kayt and Jay had all moved over to the domed climbing frame and were now sitting in a small circle inside its caged structure. Kayt was still holding tightly onto Scavenger, who rather than resisting, cuddled in and curled into a tight ball on her lap.

'I don't know,' Tobias replied. 'But if you promise not to freak out and you can keep a secret, I know someone who might.'

Tobias didn't really want to reveal Hex, especially in front of Jay, but he also felt like he owed the other boy some kind of explanation. After all, Jay had jumped in to save them.

Both Jay and Kayt nodded acceptance to the deal so Tobias pulled the teardrop gem from under his t-shirt and laid it down in the centre of their huddle.

'What is it?' Jay asked as soon as the object touched the dirt. He even moved to prod it with a finger but flinched back in shock when the purple mists shifted into the shape of a face and Hex spoke.

'I am Hexalbion Ignatius Grimm and I do not appreciate being referred to as an it.'

'What the hell?' was all Jay could manage in reply, so Hex continued.

'I do not agree with this Tobias. I know you think you can trust the girl, but you hardly know this boy. Even you must admit, your encounters with him have not been particularly pleasant ones.'

'I know,' Tobias replied. 'But he saved us. Besides, I think that thing must have been after me. If it was, I'm the one who put them in danger in the first place.'

'Oh it most certainly will have been after you. After all, that beast was a Vikessan Shadow Hunter. The only time they are ever released is to track down valuable targets, like yourself.'

'Oi,' Jay interrupted loudly. 'I don't know what's going on here but if you don't start explaining, I'm going to have to beat it out of you.' Both he and Kayt were looking particularly confused, but while Kayt remained surprisingly quiet and calm, Jay was beginning to look rather angry.

'It's a long story,' Tobias replied.

'You had better get started then.'

'Fine. I'll do my best to explain.'

So Tobias began at the beginning. He told both Jay and Kayt all about what had happened to him. About being snatched from his room, being locked up in the Underlands, meeting Scavenger and then his terrifying escape with the help of Hex. He even told them all about the Witch Mother and her Demons. What he didn't reveal however, were the details about Tyringar and the possibility that he himself may be the reincarnation of one of the denizens of those dark realms.

'What rubbish,' Jay spat out when Tobias had finished but Kayt turned on the older boy with a hard stare.

'Don't be a Jerk Jay,' she scolded him.

'What? You really believe all that nonsense?'

'Why not? Look at what you have just seen. That creature definitely wasn't anything natural was it.'

'I know but…'

'And you have Hex and Scavenger here. They prove some of it.'

'Yeah but…'

'So why can't it be true? Remember when the news was full of missing kids? None of them were found, and this would certainly explain that. My dad always says the obvious answer is usually right and…'

'Okay, okay,' Jay interrupted. He was clearly getting impatient, but at least he didn't look quite as angry. 'Let's just say wimpy is telling the truth. That still doesn't explain what that thing was. Or why it was here.'

Jay slumped back against the bars of the climbing frame and looked from Kayt to Tobias for some kind of answer but it was Hex who replied.

'If I may speak?'

'Sure why not. Let's hear what the talking rock has to say.'

'My name is Hexalbion, child. You would do well to remember that.'

Jay scoffed in response, but when Hex did not continue, and it became apparent that he was waiting for something more, Jay begrudgingly offered a, 'fine. Let's hear what Hexalbion has to say. Happy now?'

'Thank you. Now, like I said, that beast was a Shadow Hunter and I know of only one Master who makes use of them. Dvesh, the Lord of Malice and ruler of Vikessa.'

'But why would this Dvesh send them after me? Tobias asked.

'He is an ally of the Witch Mother. I would imagine that she has recruited Dvesh to aid in her search for you. Especially since her own connection to this world has been severed.'

'So what do we do?' Tobias asked.

'That is not an easy question to answer. Especially when we still know so little. Clearly there must be another Gate, and it is most likely one that connects to Vikessa. If we can find that Gate, we might be able to close it.'

'Then will I be safe?'

'It will buy us some time to figure something else out.'

'So what do we do?' Kayt asked eagerly, looking at Hex's stone.

'We?' The shock was clear in Tobias' voice. 'I'm not putting you in danger too.'

'I'm your friend Tobias. I want to help. Besides, you aren't putting me in danger. I am. It's my decision and my dad always says there is no point arguing with me when I make my mind up so you shouldn't even try.'

'Well if Freako is helping then so am I,' Jay added.

'Seriously, you are both far safer if you just stay out of this and stay away from me.'

But it was no good. Both Jay and Kayt just stared straight at him with determined looks on their faces. The kind of looks which told him that no matter how much he argued or how much he complained, nothing was going to change their minds.

'Fine,' he said at last. 'But promise me you will run at the first sign of any danger.'

'Promise,' they both replied, almost in unison.

Tobias shook his head in frustration and turned his attention back to Hex. 'Okay, what do we do?'

'Well first thing first, if you are all determined to get yourselves involved, you need to understand the danger. Shadow Hunters are experts at tracking their targets but they are rarely alone. Despite their skill, they are still animals and a Shadow Hunter will almost always have a handler.'

'If it's just an animal can't we just kill it?' Jay asked dismissively.

'Do not be a fool,' Hex hissed back at him. 'You might think you are strong and tough, but these things are nothing like anything in your world. They will rip the flesh from your bones and scatter your innards across the ground. They will show no mercy, no remorse. They will slaughter you without a care and fight over which gets to devour your remains.'

'So we can't kill it then?'

Hex sighed loudly. 'No. No mortal could hope to kill it.'

Tobias looked from Jay to Kayt as Hex ranted. Jay was shifting nervously but still doing his best to maintain an *I don't care* face. Kayt, on the other hand, had gone pale. Small beads of sweat were forming on her brow and she was cuddling Scavenger even tighter.

'Now,' Hex continued, 'The handler is the true danger. The Shadow Hunter is the muscle but its handler is the brain. It will be cunning and it will be hidden, but if we are fast and careful, we might be able to find the Gate and figure out a plan before the handler knows what we are doing.'

'How do we do that?' Tobias asked.

'If it is indeed a Gate with Vikessa, it should be easy to identify. Vikessa is a place of misery and despair far beyond that of any other realm.'

'Even more than the Underlands?' Tobias found the idea both terrifying and hard to believe.

'It is a very different kind of despair. While the Underlands contain suffering and evil, Vikessa is it's physical embodiment. A person would feel fear and desperation in the Underlands but in Vikessa, the feeling of utter hopelessness would permeate their very being. Thankfully, this is what helps us find it's Gate. You see, any link that Vikessa has with another realm is a place where it's toxic energies can seep out and taint the area around it. We just need to find such a place.'

'How do we do that?' Kayt asked, her voice holding a definite quiver.

'It's okay if you want to go home,' Tobias told her. 'I understand.'

'No. I want to help.'

'Are you sure?'

'Yeah. I'm sure. I'm not going anywhere.'

Tobias smiled at Kayt and she gave a nervous smile back. Jay on the other hand just rolled his eyes and coughed loudly.

'Barf,' he said mockingly. 'What a pair of sissies. Now can we please get on with this. How do we find this Gate thingy?'

'It will be a place of permanent and unnatural shadow. A place where nothing grows, no animals tread and even being in its presence invokes a sense of deep sorrow.'

'School!' Jay blurted out abruptly.

'Don't be daft Jay,' Kayt replied. 'This is serious.'

'I am being serious. The haunted hallway.'

'Please Jay.'

'Honestly. In the old science block. Haven't you heard the stories?'

Kayt was looking increasingly aggravated, but from what Tobias could tell, Jay was serious.

'What stories?' He asked.

'Well apparently loads of strange stuff kept happening. Plants kept dying, lights wouldn't work, teachers kept getting ill, and kids kept having accidents. According to one story a teacher even had a breakdown after claiming that he saw goblins.'

Kayt shook her head in disbelief. 'I've never heard any of this.'

'I'm not surprised. This was all before I even started at the school. They haven't used the rooms down there in years.'

'We should check it out,' Tobias suggested, but Jay shook his head.

'There's just one problem with that.'

'What?'

'We used to dare each other to sneak in there, so the school has locked it all up.'

'So how can we get in?'

'I can pick locks,' Kayt said and both Jay and Tobias turned to face her in obvious shock.

Kayt glanced back at them, turning her head from one to the other and turning such a bright shade of red that it almost drowned out her freckles. 'What?' She said quietly. 'My dad taught me.'

'Your dad taught you to pick locks?' Jay asked.

'Yeah. It was fun,' Kayt replied as if that explained everything. When no one spoke her face turned even more crimson. 'All I am saying is that I can pick the lock if you need me to. It's not a big deal or anything. I'm just saying that I can do it.'

'Well great, I guess.' Tobias replied eventually. 'If you get me in there, we should be able to work out if it's the Gate or not.'

'Awesome,' Kayt replied.

'Sounds good to me,' Jay added.

'What's the worst that could happen?' said Hex with just a hint of mockery.

Tobias looked at them all. He had escaped the Underlands with just Hex and Scavenger. Now all he had to do was figure out how to close a single Gate, and this time he had two more to help him.

'Okay,' he said. 'I guess we will do this on Monday then.'

Chapter 9

Though Tobias tried his best to get an early night on the Sunday, sleep did not come easily. Thanks to his nerves, he found himself turning back to a number of his old habits. He checked his window to make sure it was securely locked, peered beneath his bed to be certain it was clear, and pulled his stool up in front of his wardrobe to block it shut. He even locked the new latch on his bedroom door.

Finally, he turned the handle of his old windup torch several times to build a charge and laid in his bed with it clutched tight to his chest. It felt strange to be thinking of all the old monsters which used to plague his imagination before his time in the Underlands, but that night, his brain simply wouldn't stop churning with the fevered imaginings of beasts like howlers and lurkers.

These thoughts even managed to creep into his nightmares and once sleep did take him, he suffered several dreams of dark shadowy entities crawling up the building's exterior and tapping on his windows. Most of these dreams were vague and bled into one another, but one stood out among the rest. It was clear and distinct.

Tobias was curled up beneath his covers when he heard a soft rapping at his window. Pulling the duvet tighter around his head, he attempted to ignore the sound, but the more he tried to block it out, the louder it got. It grew from a gentle and distant clicking, to a louder and rhythmic tap, before becoming a thunderous banging. Then it stopped.

Tobias listened intently from beneath his covers but the sound was completely gone. All he could hear was the sound of his own breathing. Feeling strangely compelled to investigate the sudden lack of noise, Tobias peeled back his covers and looked over to the window.

Peering through the dark glass, he tried to make out any details of the outside world, but there was nothing there. Absolutely nothing. There was no light, no distant shapes of nearby buildings, no stars or even a moon. It was just total and impenetrable darkness.

Uncertain what strange magic made him do it, Tobias pushed back his bedding and climbed to his feet. He stepped closer to the window and strained his eyes, but still nothing could be seen.

'Hello Tobias,' said a voice behind him. It was a quiet voice which spoke in a measured tone and was so slow that each word seemed to be dragged out over several seconds.

Feeling the hairs on the back of his neck prickle, Tobias slowly turned around to look at the robed man with no face. His white, featureless skin stared back and his blood soaked hands once again reached up to Tobias' eyes.

'I'm coming for you,' said the voice as the tiny serrated teeth bit down hard.

Tobias awoke with a jolt and a yelp which disturbed Scavenger and caused the small rodent to jump himself.

'Sorry,' Tobias said as Scavenger jumped up onto the bed and cuddled into his chest. 'Just another bad dream.'

Tobias looked over at his clock. It was still only half past two. Far too early to be getting up, but there was no way he was going to be able to get back to sleep now. So, turning his lamp on and pressing the button which flared his torch into life, he waited for morning.

By the time his alarm finally erupted into life, Tobias was already getting up. The sun hadn't even risen high enough to peek above the rooftops when he had climbed out of bed and begun to dress in his school uniform.

After straightening his tie and folding down his shirt collar, he hung Hex around his neck and tucked the stone beneath his jumper.

'I take it you are still planning on looking for the Gate then?' Hex asked with a hint of genuine surprise.

'I need to. We need to know what we are up against.'

'And you are still including Kayt and Jay in this?'

'They want to help. I take it you don't agree with it?'

'I think that they will only bring you trouble.'

'Kayt is my friend.'

'Exactly, you don't have the luxury of friends. Not while the Witch Mother is still after you. Besides, you can hardly consider Jay to be your friend. I don't even understand why he wants to help.'

'Neither do I,' Tobias admitted. 'But he seemed genuine and I could do with all the help I can get.'

'People are a liability. They are a weakness which your enemies can exploit. You are better off without them.'

Once again, Tobias could feel his anger and frustration rising. 'So I guess I should just abandon you then should I?'

'That is different,' Hex replied. 'My knowledge can help you. Not to mention we still have a deal to complete.'

'They are helping,' Tobias spat. 'Get used to it or keep quiet. I'm sick of arguing with you.'

'Fine. Just don't say I didn't warn you.'

Tobias sighed loudly and turned his attention back to his mirror. His face was flushed and his brow creased in a frown which betrayed his frustration. Allowing himself a moment to calm, he pressed his fingers to the picture of his parents.

'Love you,' he murmured.

He was just about to leave his room when he stopped and turned back to his bed. Something was tickling at the back of his mind like an itch he just couldn't reach.

Crawling onto all fours, he reached under and pulled out a bundle of tightly wrapped cloth before unwrapping it to reveal the long slender blade of Fear Bane.

Just the sight of the focus sent an odd wave of shivers through his body. A giddy mix of fear and excitement which he had to fight down as he held the weapon.

He hadn't unwrapped Fear Bane since he had hidden it under his bed. That was just two days after escaping the Underlands. A part of him had always wanted to take it back out. He had craved the sensation that came with holding the focus, but Tobias had always resisted in the hopes that he would never need it again. Now it looked like those hopes had been dashed.

Pushing the weapon back into it's bundle, he stowed it in his bag and headed out of his room to finish preparing for school.

'Morning Toby,' his uncle greeted him with a smile.

'Morning,' Tobias replied.

This was one of the remarkably rare instances where his uncle had one of his better days. A day when he not only found the strength to get himself up, but also the will to wash, dress and even prepare breakfast himself. In this case there were sausages in the oven and he was buttering a small stack of bread.

'Breakfast won't be long. I've already fed Scavenger.'

Tobias looked over to Scavenger's bowl and sure enough, it was piled high with an un-appetising, dull grey mush, which was presumably meant to be cat food. Scavenger did not look happy but he was dutifully eating anyway.

'So are you excited for another week at school?' his uncle continued as he put the butter away and pulled the tray of sausages out of the oven.

'Yeah. I guess.'

'You know I'm proud of you don't you.'

The words took Tobias by surprise and when he looked up, there was a definite wetness to his uncle's eyes.

'I know,' was all he could think to say.

'I haven't been the best guardian since, well, you know. Hell I haven't been much of a guardian at all. But I'm still proud of you. I know your mum and dad would be too.'

Wiping tears away from his face with the back of a sleeve, his uncle pushed two of the sausages in between bread and passed the plate over to Tobias.

'I know it will take time, but we are getting better aren't we?' he asked as Tobias took the plate.

'I guess,' Tobias replied. He wasn't entirely sure what to say or how he felt, but he could tell by the way the man's shoulders slumped, that this was not the response his uncle had wanted.

Tobias forced a smile and met his uncle's eyes. 'Sorry,' he said. 'It's still hard, but things are better.'

His uncle wiped yet another tear away and smiled back. 'Thanks,'

After that, they ate their breakfast in silence before Tobias finished packing his things. He checked he had his school books, checked that Fear Bane was still safely stowed away and then bundled a blanket into the top of his bag so that he could take Scavenger.

'I might need your support today,' he told the chubby pink rodent as he lifted him into his backpack.

Finally, as he left the apartment, his uncle gave him an awkward hug and told him to have a good time.

In a strange way Tobias felt guilty as he left. Despite these occasional good days, he still knew his uncle needed a lot of help, and that he was the only real consistency which existed in his uncle's life.

'I still don't see why you care about him so much,' Hex said as they jogged along the streets towards Jay's house.

'He's my uncle.'

'You keep saying that but I still don't understand. After everything he did to you, why does that still matter? If he was my uncle and he treated me like that, I would have abandoned him a long time ago. And that would be if he was lucky.'

'Well it doesn't really work like that in this world. I need an adult or I go into care. Besides, I can't abandon him. He is trying his best and he needs me.'

'Well I still don't understand,' Hex said as they finally rounded a corner with the meeting point just up ahead.

It was still quite early but Jay was already leaning against the wall at the end of his driveway. He was wearing a heavy leather jacket and was swinging a thick wooden stick through the air like he was batting at invisible targets.

'Oi Wimp! Over here!' he called out when he noticed Tobias appear.

'He is another one you would be better off without.' Hex muttered.

'I don't know,' Tobias replied as he walked over. 'It's not like he can't handle himself.'

'You really think someone like that could have survived what you went through?'

'Maybe. Who knows. Anyway, shut up about it. He is here and for some reason he wants to help so let's not upset him.'

'Where's Freako?' Jay asked when Tobias was close enough.

'Her name is Kayt.'

'Fine. Where is Kayt?'

'I don't know. She must still be on her way.'

'Well just to be clear, I am not here for her, or for you. I'm only here to show those cat things who is boss.' He swung the stick through the air for added emphasis.

'Okay but you know we're not going to fight unless we have to, don't you?'

'Yeah, yeah.'

Tobias looked up at Jay's face. He was acting dismissive but Tobias recognised the telltale signs of fear. The tense muscles, shifting eyes, and guarded stance were all very familiar. He said nothing though. Jay was clearly putting on a front and he was unlikely to appreciate anybody questioning it.

'Sorry I'm late,' Came Kayt's voice as she rushed over to join them. 'My dad insisted I had a good breakfast before I left the house. I'm not sure cereal is all that good but it's what he gave me so I guess it can't be that bad. I think he wants to meet you by the way Tobias. He said that you sound like a really nice boy and you have to come over for tea or something. Anyway, did I say that I'm sorry that I'm late?'

As Kayt spoke, Tobias felt something in his backpack begin squirming excitedly. Grinning, he pulled the bag around to the front and unzipped the top. As soon as he did, Scavenger's head popped out and looked over at Kayt with an excited squeak.

Kayt scratched Scavenger behind the ear and looked up at Tobias. 'So what's the plan?'

'Well this is just a fact finding mission. We need to get in there, and if it really is the Gate, see if there are any clues as to how we can close it. I figured we could all meet outside the science block at dinner and go from there.'

'Do you think those hunter things might be there?'

'With luck they will remain hidden while so many people are around.' Hex replied.

The sudden disembodied voice made Kayt jump backwards and stumble slightly. 'I'll never get used to that,' she said as she regained her balance.

The three of them walked the rest of the way to school in silence until they were just one street away. That was when Jay broke away from them and moved on ahead.

'No offence,' he called back over his shoulder, 'but I can't be seen with you two weirdos. See you at lunch.'

Chapter 10

Lunch took longer to arrive than Tobias could ever have imagined. The entire day just seemed to drag, each minute slowly edging its way into the next. He found it difficult to concentrate on his classes. He constantly had to drag himself back into reality after drifting off into yet another daydream about what horrors might be waiting for him in the haunted hallway.

Kayt was not faring much better and her usual chatty demeanor had faded into a very distant and uncharacteristic silence. The only time she seemed to perk up at all was in between classes. That was when the two of them would sneak off to one side and give Scavenger some fresh air and a snack.

Maths was the last challenge before lunchtime and it wasn't Tobias' favourite subject at the best of times.

Mr Leach, the cantankerous old teacher who spent his time striding up and down the middle of the room, peering down at everyone over a long hooked nose, was a particularly difficult teacher to like.

He enjoyed making life hard for his students, presenting them with problems far beyond their capabilities and taking great pleasure in watching them squirm.

He also had a particular fondness for punishments and was a great believer in stripping students of their privileges for even the slightest infraction. Barely a maths class went by without someone getting detention, and this time Tobias was his target of choice.

'Mr. Crow,' he said when he noticed that Tobias' attention had wavered. 'Since you have clearly been listening very intently, maybe you could answer this one.'

Mr. Leach rounded on Tobias' table and moved in behind him. Tobias could feel the man's beady eyes staring at his back. His mind instantly conjured a mental image of the teacher's tall crooked frame leaning over like a vulture, his thin lips curled into a malicious sneer.

'What is the square root of 49?'

Tobias' mind was blank. He wasn't even sure he had been taught about square roots. He looked over to Kayt, but with Mr. Leach looming so close, she didn't dare meet his gaze.

'I don't…' Tobias began but he was immediately cut short by a whisper from under his jumper.

'7,' Hex said.

Tobias repeated the answer.

Though there was a momentary silence which let Tobias know he must be right, Mr Leach offered no congratulations. He wanted to catch Tobias out, and despite him getting one question right, Mr Leach still wasn't deterred.

'Okay, Mr. Crow,' the teacher said. 'What is the square root of 81?'

'9,' Hex whispered.

'9,' Tobias repeated.

This earned him a hiss of frustration from Mr. Leach before the teacher began firing out number after number. Each time Tobias repeated what Hex told him.

'36?'

'6.'

'64?'

'8.'

'121?'

'11.'

'Okay,' said Mr Leach, a hint of anger creeping into his voice. 'Since you are so clever, let us try some harder ones shall we. What about the square root of 529?'

'23?' Tobias repeated after Hex.

It was a fast response and he knew the answer had surprised Mr. Leach because not only did he not respond straight away, but he also failed to chastise the rest of the class when they began whispering loudly to one another.

'Well aren't you the little genius,' Mr Leach said at last. He leaned in closer and placed his hands on Tobias' shoulders. 'Okay genius, what is the square root of 40?'

Tobias didn't reply immediately because Hex had gone silent. Sweat beaded on Tobias' brow and it felt like Mr Leach's grip on his shoulders was tightening in anticipation of his victory.

'6.3246,' Hex whispered, but he sounded uncertain.

'6.3246,' Tobias repeated.

There was a pause and the whole room fell into hushed silence. The sweat trickled down the side of Tobias' nose and Mr Leach squeezed just a little bit harder at Tobias' shoulders before letting go and storming over to the front of the classroom.

Clattering through the contents of his desk drawer he ripped out a small grey calculator and hammered at the buttons.

'Quite the little smarty pants aren't we, Mr. Crow?' he hissed after seeing the answer displayed on the plastic device.

Turning to face the rest of the class he added, 'Since we clearly have a maths whiz in the class, there will be a test tomorrow. I expect you all to score as well as Mr. Crow,'

The whole class groaned in reply but Tobias just felt a wave of relief as the ordeal came to an end and the bell for lunch finally rang.

Neither he or Kayt had any interest in food and immediately rushed off to meet Jay.

'Well that was impressive,' Kayt said as they walked at a swift pace towards the science block.

'Yeah, but only thanks to Hex,' Tobias replied before pulling the stone out from beneath his clothes. 'I never knew you were so good at maths.'

'Mathematics is universal across all realms,' Hex said as if that answered everything.

'Well it was still very impressive.'

'Thank you,' Hex replied smugly as they rounded the corner and the science block loomed up in front of them.

The building itself was a long and narrow three story structure which was pressed up close to the school's perimeter.

They only had to wait a minute before Jay joined them. He was still wearing his jacket but he had turned the collar up and was dipping his head down low as if hiding. Tobias couldn't help but think that his efforts to remain unseen, only made him stand out even more.

'wimp. Freeko,' he greeted them.

'Jay,' Tobias replied.

'Well are we ready or what?'

'What if there are teachers in there?' Kayt asked.

'Don't worry. I've asked around and the teachers won't have dinner anywhere near the haunted hallway. Apparently it smells funny, but no one has figured out why. Do you think it could be because of this Gate?'

'Well isn't he the sharp one?' mocked Hex.

Tobias ignored Hex's jibe and thankfully, so did Jay. 'Let's just get on with this before someone sees us.'

'Okay, let's go.'

Tobias led the way inside the building, ducking in through the main doors, creeping past the stairwell and through the corridor beyond. They passed doors to the boys and girls toilets as well as a storeroom, but no classrooms. They were all on the other side of the locked double doors which blocked their progress just a short distance away.

Checking over his shoulder to make certain no one was around, Tobias turned to Kayt. 'Can you get us in?'

Kayt nodded 'I feel like a bank robber.' she said with a huge smile. Then, pulling some thin metal strips from her pocket, she began working on the lock. It only took a few seconds before there was a soft click.

'Impressive,' Jay said with a nod and a smile in Kayt's direction.

'Right, wait here and keep watch,' Tobias told them both as he slipped in through the doorway.

Chapter 11

The Haunted Hallway definitely lived up to its name. It was long and dark with metal lockers lining both walls. The only illumination came from thin tendrils of light creeping in through the glass panels of classroom doors.

Tobias placed his backpack down on the ground and unzipped it so that Scavenger could hop out. A glint of metal also caught his eye as the handle of Fear Bane poked out from its wrapping. Resisting the urge to touch the weapon, to draw it out and feel its power, Tobias took a deep breath and pulled the bundled cloth back over. He might need it soon but until then, he would not give into temptation.

Feeling as ready as he ever could, he gave Scavenger a small smile and then crept slowly onwards down the hallway. Scavenger stayed close at his heels.

As the two of them moved forward a familiar sensation began seeping back into Tobias' bones. It caused his hands to quiver ever so slightly and his skin to become cold and clammy.

He immediately recognised it as the trembling feeling of fear, and though it was something he had been feeling less and less in recent months, it still came as naturally as it ever had before. It was different now though. Now his fear was not something he considered a weakness. It was his power. His weapon against the darkness.

Steeling his resolve against the oppressive gloom of the place, Tobias swung his backpack onto his shoulders and edged further down the hall.

Inky blankets of shadow swept in from the walls and plunged the opposite end of the hallway in complete darkness. At the same time the lockers loomed inwards, practically oozing evil intent. The whole thing conjured an eerie scene, which was only made worse by the cold, dank smell which permeated the air.

Ignoring the churning sense of unease which was building deep in his stomach, Tobias continued to walk steadily down the hallway until he came to the first classroom.

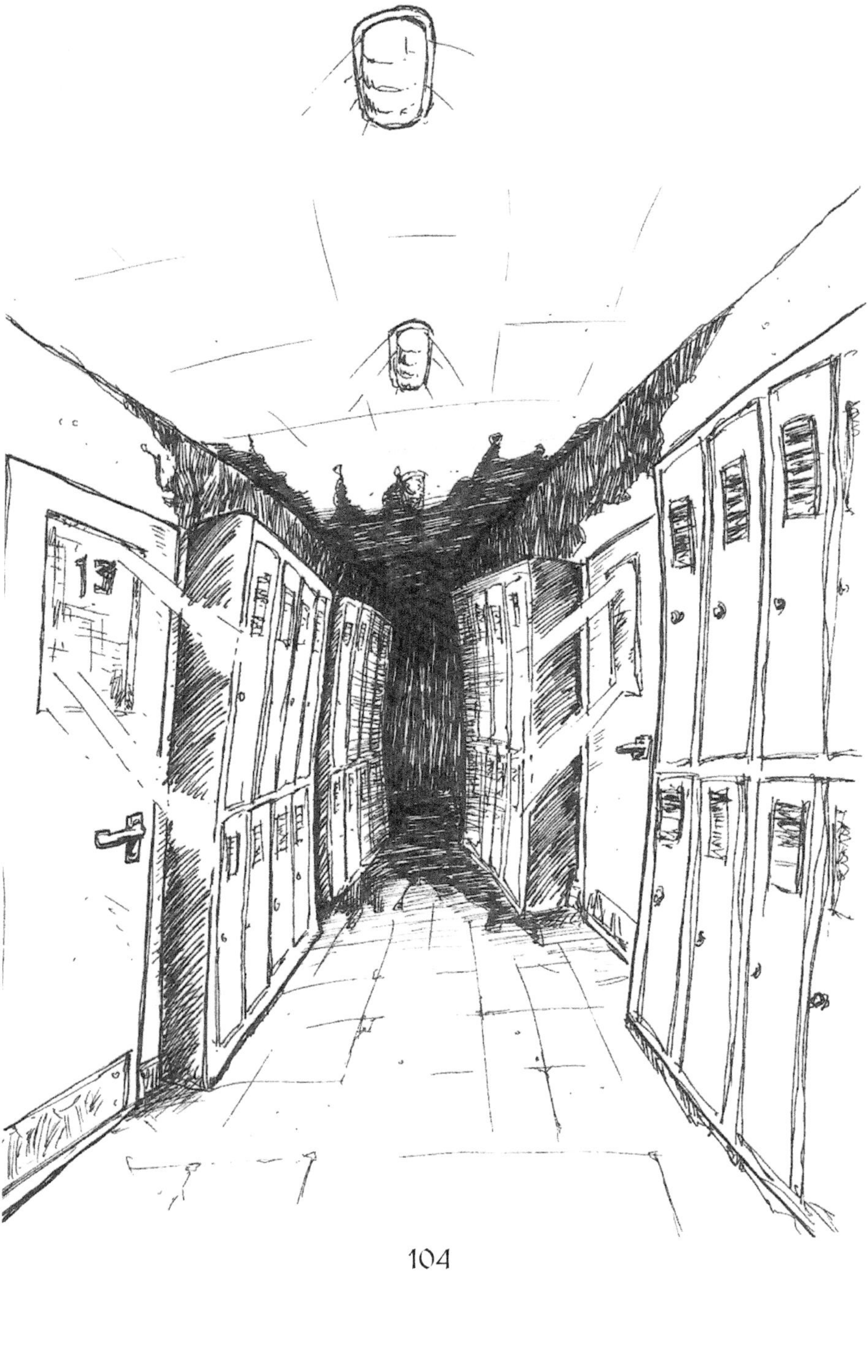
13

Pushing the door gently ajar, he squeezed his body through and scanned the room.

Large wooden counters lined the walls, holding nothing but the dust and grime of disuse. Tables and chairs sat motionless and without purpose, and a wide window, which could have filled the room with light, was instead obscured by heavy fabric blinds.

The room looked like it had not been used in years. Yet something was standing in the darkness. A small yet humanoid shape which seemed to blend in with the shadows so perfectly that it was almost invisible. Only a vague outline could be seen but it was definitely there. The shape was hunched in the corner close to the open door of the classroom's only cupboard. It was watching Tobias.

'There is something there,' Hex whispered and Tobias felt Scavenger's claws grip tightly to his trouser leg.

Still the shape watched him.

Gingerly, Tobias raised his arm and began reaching towards his backpack. He didn't want to make any sudden moves but he also didn't want to be unarmed in case the creature attacked.

His fingers crept up to the edge of the open zip and felt their way along to the soft bundle that wrapped the blade. He was about to ease it out when a sharp whistle pierced the silence and everything erupted into sudden chaos.

'Oi! Tobias!' Jay's voice called out.

'Quick!' Kayt added.

The creature stiffened and darted sideways out of sight, behind the closet door. At the same time the strip lights in the hallway outside flickered and buzzed into life. One of them popped loudly as it glowed momentarily before going dark once more.

'Hey!' a voice yelled angrily. 'What are you lot up to?'

'Nothing Mr. Leach,' Kayt replied.

'You aren't allowed down here! Who is in there?'

'No one Sir, it's just me and Jay. The door was open and we just wanted to have a look. You know what they say about curiosity.'

'It killed the cat?' Jay sounded legitimately confused.

'Well, yeah, but they also say that it is the wick in the candle of learning.'

'Really? I've never heard anyone say that.'

'My dad told me someone named William Ward said it. He also said that …'

'That's enough!' Mr Leach snapped, silencing them both. 'I'll find out for myself.'

The door to the hallway creaked open and the bony form of Mr Leach stepped through. 'Okay,' He yelled. 'I know someone is in here. Come out now.'

Tobias quickly scooped up Scavenger and bundled him out of sight into his backpack before stepping into the hallway. He gave one last glance back at the classroom cupboard but there was no sign of the creature he had seen, and with the light now cascading in, it looked like an ordinary brown wooden door.

'Well, well, well. If it isn't the little genius, Mr. Crow.' Mr. Leach's voice was dripping with contempt as Tobias emerged in front of him. 'I am sure that with your great intellect you can furnish me with a perfectly reasonable explanation as to why you are here.'

Tobias looked down at the floor and tried his best to look apologetic. 'Like Kayt said, the door was open and I was just wanting to see what was down there.'

'So you thought you would just wander around school buildings unsupervised and in the dark?'

'I'm sorry Mr. Leach. I didn't know we weren't allowed to go in.'

'And yet you had your friends stand watch.'

'He's got us there,' said Jay.

'Shush,' scolded Kayt.

'Indeed I do Mr. Adler. Indeed I do. Now, I will be contacting your parents immediately and assuming that they do not object, I think an after school detention might be in order. Just to make sure you know to ignore your curiosities in future.'

Evidently, none of their parents or guardians had objected to the detention, because when the end of school came around, all three of them found themselves sitting in a small classroom sharpening pencils and organising text books.

'So what happened?' Kayt asked the instant Mr. Leach left the room. 'Did you find anything?'

'There was definitely something there. It was some kind of creature but I didn't get a good look at it.'

'So what do we do?'

'I don't know. We need to get back in there, but it has to be when we have more time.'

'We have time now,' Jay said as he tossed a text book across the room like a frisbee. He grinned as it crashed into the wall and fell to the floor.

'I don't know if you have realised, but we are in detention.' Kayt replied.

'I know, but think about it. School is over, most of the teachers have gone home and the science block will be completely empty.'

'He has a point,' Tobias admitted.

Kayt turned on Tobias with a stern look which caused her eyes to narrow beneath her glasses.

'We are in detention.' she said again, this time pointing a freshly sharpened pencil at him to punctuate her point.

'I know but…'

'But nothing. We can't just go wandering through the school. We have to stay here and wait till we are allowed to go home. What happens if something goes wrong and we aren't back in time?'

'Mr Leach will be mad,' Jay replied with a dismissive grunt. 'So what? He is always mad.'

'It's not just Mr. Leach though. How do you think my Dad would feel if I just went missing? Especially when I'm meant to be in detention. If we are going to do this, we need more than just half an hour. We need a day at least.'

'Kayt's right,' Tobias said. 'We need to sneak in on the weekend. When school is closed.'

'That's not what I said.'

'It makes sense though. We would have the whole day and no one would be around to catch us.'

'I guess, but...'

'It's settled then,' Jay interrupted. 'We come back on saturday. I'll say I'm sleeping at a friend's house and if you two say the same, we will have all day and all night.'

Both Jay and Tobias looked straight at Kayt, and for a moment she met their gaze with a fixed, no-nonsense glare. Unfortunately, she couldn't maintain it for long.

'Oh okay. But Jay has to stop messing around and pull his weight.'

'Deal,' Tobias replied, not waiting to see if Jay agreed or not.

Jay just grunted before wandering around the room and picking up all the stationary he had been hurling.

Chapter 12

A low growl broke the silence of Tobias' room as he laid staring up at the ceiling on the Friday night. It was a deep vibration which echoed in the air and resonated with a predatory malice.

Certain that the noise was coming from the other side of his door, but with no clue as to what it might be, Tobias climbed out the opposite side of his bed and crouched low. Trying to be as silent as possible, his bare feet hit the floor with a soft thud. It was not carpet which greeted his feet, however, but soft wet soil.

Tobias looked down in confusion to see mud squelching up between his toes. He couldn't understand it. Why was there so much mud in his room? It didn't make any sense. Yet when he looked back up, he wasn't in his room at all. There was no door, no bed, not even walls. He was in a dense jungle of vines and branches which stretched out in all directions without end.

Tobias felt panic rising in his stomach. He was certain something unseen meant him harm, but he didn't know where he was or how he had gotten there. He had nothing to defend himself with, and without knowing where the danger was, he couldn't even find a place to hide.

The growl filled the air again. It sounded even closer this time, but there was still no way to pinpoint its direction. Tobias found himself spinning on the spot in an effort to watch all sides for any sign of movement.

A glint of movement caught his eye as something passed between two columns of nearby grass. He whirled around to face it, just in time to see a large black shape disappear from view behind the tall greenery. It was only a momentary glimpse, but it was all Tobias needed to recognise the same Shadow Hunter he had faced in the park. A fresh crimson gash marred its face where it's left eye had once been, and it's good eye shot Tobias with a glare of unbridled anger before the beast once again disappeared from view.

Tobias tried to run in the opposite direction but something else was stopping him. It had grabbed him by the shoulders and was blocking his path.

The faceless man pulled Tobias in close until he was just inches away from the featureless alabaster skin which peered out from beneath the hood of its dark grey robe. Its long fingers clutched on tight and the gnashing maws on its palms bit deep into Tobias' flesh.

As it leaned in, its slow voice whispered into Tobias ear. 'Do not worry, Tobias. I am coming for you.'

Tobias leapt backward, tripped on a branch and fell hard with the stranger still bearing down on top of him.

As he tumbled out of bed and hit the floor in a mess of limbs and blanket, it took Tobias a moment to realise it had all been a nightmare. His skin still felt cold and every muscle was tensed in anticipation of pain, but he was safe. He was sprawled out on his bedroom floor with Scavenger staring down at him from the edge of the bed.

'It's okay. Just a bad dream,' he said, reassuring himself as much as his friend.

Untangling himself from his blanket and lifting himself to his feet, Tobias clenched his eyes tight and tried to shake off the anxiety left by his dream. He could see the sun through his window and it was already starting to creep over the horizon, announcing that it was now Saturday morning. The day he was going to sneak into school and try to find the Gate.

'Well, this is it. The day we have been waiting for,' he said as he gave Scavenger a gentle pat on the head. Scavenger squeaked in reply.

Tobias didn't waste any time. He had already packed a bag with everything that he thought he might need, including his first aid kit, snacks, water, torch, and of course, Fear Bane. All he had to do now was wash, dress, eat and go.

The clothes he had chosen were the same ones that he had escaped the Underlands in. The hard wearing red jumper, brown trousers and leather boots. They had been a gift from Avesria but they were no longer as good a fit as he remembered. They seemed just a little bit too short and tight around his middle. They weren't uncomfortable though.

With the clothes was the rough cloth bag which contained some of the trinkets he had also brought back with him. He removed the bone charm which opened the Gate from the Underlands to his world. He did not want to take that anywhere it could fall into the wrong hands. He did, however, leave in the wire framed Revelare Lenses which allowed him to read the magic languages of the other Realms.

Finally, he wolfed down a bowl of porridge, took another bowl to his uncle, and then grabbed his bag to go. Hex was already hanging around his neck and Scavenger was close at his heels.

'Remember that I'm sleeping at a friend's tonight,' Tobias called out to his uncle as he ducked out of the front door. He didn't think that his uncle would ask many questions, but he didn't want to risk waiting to find out. Still, a pang of guilt gnawed in his stomach as the door clicked shut behind him. He knew Mary was going to check in on his uncle but he still felt like he was abandoning him.

'You know the creature will be expecting you now don't you?' Hex asked as Tobias sprinted down the stairs and out of the apartment block.

'I figured,' Tobias replied.

'That's it? You figured? Why do I get the feeling there is something you aren't telling me?'

Tobias ran down the street. There was a good distance between him and the park, but he was determined to cover it as quickly as he could.

'I have a plan,' he said as he slowed slightly to turn a sharp corner.

'What plan?'

'I'm going through the Gate.'

'You are what?' The sudden heightened pitch of Hex's voice betrayed his surprise. 'You can't be serious. You have no idea what is on the other side.'

'I have to do it. I have to take the fight to them.'

'Have you forgotten what we went through to escape the Underlands?'

'Of course I haven't but this is different. I have so much to lose now. I am starting to feel like I have a real family again. I have a life, friends, and I am happy for the first time in, well, ever. I cannot let all that be put at risk. I have to do this.'

'This is madness Tobias. Utter madness.'

'Look, I know this seems crazy but what other options do we have? Keep running? Keep Hiding? Keep being afraid? I can't do it anymore. I am going to go in there. I am going to get answers, and I am going to deal with the Witch Mother once and for all.'

'Tobias.' Hex took on a softer tone. 'You know that I will serve you as best I can to atone for what I did, but I have my limits and this whole endeavour is incredibly foolhardy. Not to mention, incredibly uncharacteristic of you.'

'I told you Hex, I have to protect what I've now got.'

With that Tobias rounded the final bend and emerged with the park just across the road. Both the play area and field were empty of life and the morning dew still clung to the grass.

Making his way across to the trees and bushes at the back of the park, Tobias ducked in through the branches and entered the small space of the den within. Kayt and Jay were already waiting with their own bags resting by their sides. Both of them smiled as he entered but the smiles didn't reach their eyes and they were sitting with obvious tension in their muscles. Neither of them looked comfortable and Tobias could tell that he wasn't the only one battling with the nervous worry of what was to come. All three of them had been struggling with it since Monday.

Not only had Kayt spent the week being far less chatty, but by the time Friday had arrived, she was frequently drifting off mid sentence, or losing her train of thought completely. In class, she spent most of her time staring blankly at her work and chewing on her pen.

As for Jay, his tension had grown with each day that passed. He stopped hanging around with his other friends, and became increasingly surly. By Friday, he was stalking the school corridors like an angry ogre, growling and snapping at anyone who got in his way.

'I just need you to open the doors and stand guard again.' Tobias told them. Kayt shook her head.

'We are coming with you.'

'You can't. I'm going to go through the Gate.'

'We guessed that you might, but we are ready and we are still coming with you.'

'Yeah,' Jay added. 'Why do you think we said we were sleeping out? It wasn't so we could just spend the weekend hiding in school.'

'But you can't come with me,' Tobias insisted. 'You have no idea how dangerous it is.'

'That's true,' Kayt replied. 'But if it is half as dangerous as you say, you will need us to watch your back. Besides, this isn't a discussion. We are telling you that we are coming and that is that.'

'This may all be rather irrelevant anyway,' Hex interrupted. 'If we can not open the Gate, no one is going through.'

Tobias looked from Kayt to Jay. Both had their faces set in a stern glare which told him that there was little point arguing with them right now.

'Fine,' he said with an exasperated sigh. 'Let's just see what happens.'

Chapter 13

It only took ten minutes for Jay to guide the group along a small handful of streets and up a narrow walkway. On their right was the brick wall which formed the schools boundary, while on the left tall wooden fences separated them from gardens which ran up the back of a row of houses.

Kayt looked up at the brick wall with obvious confusion on her face. 'How are we supposed to get over?'

'It's easy,' Jay replied. 'We just jump up on that bin over there, use the lamppost to reach that ledge and pull ourselves over the wall.'

'Okay. But I still don't understand how you know a way into school?' Kayt put strong emphasis on the word 'into'. Tobias was also confused why a boy like Jay would want to break into a place he generally tried to avoid.

'It's always good to have a way in where no one can see you,' Jay replied as if the answer should be obvious to them. 'What's the point of sneaking out if you just get caught trying to get back.'

'I guess that makes sense,' Kayt said as she turned back to the wall. 'And you are sure no one will see us.'

'No one has ever caught me before, and that was when the school was full of teachers. Come on. What are we waiting for?'

With that Jay was off. He climbed up onto the large black bin, wrapped an arm around a nearby lamppost, and used it to swing a leg up to a small ledge that had been formed when some of the brickwork had crumbled away. From there he could heave himself up onto the top of the wall and drop over the other side.

Tobias and Kayt looked at each other with an awkward shrug before attempting to copy. It was not as easy as Jay made it look and Tobias had to make three separate attempts to reach the ledge before he finally found purchase. He also struggled to muster the strength needed to pull himself up the last foot to the top, but with a grunt of effort, he managed to drag himself over.

Kayt dropped down next to him. She looked as red and flushed as he felt.

'You two are such girls.' Jay said as they caught their breath.

'I am a girl,' Kayt replied.

'You know what I mean.'

Tobias ignored them both and looked back to see Scavenger appear at the top of the wall and bound effortlessly down to land by his feet. There was a small chirp of pride from the rodent as he puffed out his chest and stood as tall as he could manage.

'See,' Jay said, 'He isn't a girl. At least, I don't think he is.'

'I'm pretty sure he is a boy,' Tobias replied between panting.

'Definitely more of a boy than either of you too,' Jay laughed.

'Again, I am a girl,' Kayt replied impatiently.

'Yeah, yeah. Anyway, let's get going.'

Jay led them across the school field and to the back of the old science block. From there, they skirted around the edge of the building until they came to the main doors. It felt strange to be in the school when it was so empty and quiet, and Tobias kept expecting a crowd of teachers or pupils to emerge from around a corner at any minute.

'I got this.' Kayt pulled her lockpicks out of her pocket and approached the door. A few minutes and a soft click later, she pushed it ajar and moved inside. Both Tobias and Jay pulled out torches before following.

'You are way too good at that,' Jay said once they were inside the building.

Kayt looked back with a sheepish grin. 'Thanks. I've been practicing all week. Now shine one of the torches over here so I can open the next one.'

Tobias stepped forward and shone his torch towards the doors which lead into the Haunted Hallway. To his surprise, however, the doors weren't actually locked and were hanging slightly ajar.

'That's probably not good,' Kayt said, putting her lockpicks away.

'I doubt it,' Tobias replied. 'Best let me go first.

He handed his torch to Kayt and pulled Fear Bane out from his bag. The cold metal of the handle immediately warmed to his touch, and he felt a sense of power surge into his body. It was like a tingle of excitement which ran up his arm and down his spine.

Looking back at Jay, Kayt and Scavenger, he took a deep breath and moved quietly into the hallway beyond. The others followed close behind.

'I don't feel right,' Jay whispered.

Tobias stopped and looked back at both him and Kayt. He could see their fear now. It was a dense orange smoke which swirled around their bodies. Other than that, however, they looked fine.

'What do you mean?' He asked.

'I don't know. I just feel weird. Kind of sad and tired at the same time.'

'That's the energy of Vikessa seeping through the Gate,' Hex explained. He too was keeping his voice low.

'You don't need to go any further,' Tobias told both his friends.

Kayt just shook her head and took another step forward. 'I'll be fine. I'm not going back now.'

'Me too,' Jay added.

Nodding, Tobias turned back to look down the hallway and began moving forward once again.

It was exactly how he remembered it. The darkness crept in from every corner and snaked across the floor as if it was alive. The lockers still loomed like silent but menacing sentinels. The air was thick and stale, and the only light was what little could pierce in through the glass panels of the classroom doors.

The others all huddled in close around him as he edged towards the first classroom. Pushing the door aside, they filed in and looked over at the cupboard on the far side.

'What on earth is that?' Jay said as he stared in open shock.

Where there had previously been an empty stationary cupboard, there was now a swirling mass of tiny grey particles. It filled the doorframe like a mini tornado, whipping up all the dust and debris of the floor into an almost solid wall which obscured the space beyond.

'That's the Gate.' Hex replied, then with a voice full of urgency, he added, 'Hide quickly.'

Tobias bolted for cover behind one of the desks and threw himself to the ground. Scavenger rushed in beside him and tucked into his body. Kayt and Jay also darted across the room, but they went the opposite direction and ducked down behind the teachers desk. Both hurriedly switched off their torches just in time as something emerged from the Gate.

Tobias felt his breath catch in his throat and his grip tighten on Fear Bane as the large sleek shape of the Shadow Hunter stalked forward. It sniffed at the air and surveyed the scene with its one good eye before making its way into the middle of the room.

The wound where its left eye had once been looked as fresh as it had in Tobias' nightmare. A second deep cut ran across its front left shoulder. Neither injury seemed to phase it though, and when it turned its head in Tobias' direction, he was sure that it had seen him. Thankfully, instead of lunging in, or pouncing over the desk, the Shadow Hunter just turned back to the classroom door and lazily padded out into the hallway.

Tobias watched it go and waited for a count of ten before slowly lifting himself up and stepping out from his hiding place.

'Is it gone?' Kayt asked when both she and Jay also emerged.

'I think so,' Tobias replied.

He looked back at the cupboard. The Gate was already starting to lose some of its substance and dust was beginning to settle once again as the spiral of wind started to fade.

'I need to go.'

'We need to go,' Kayt corrected him.

'Seriously, you should stay here. It will be really dangerous in there and I might not be able to get back.'

'We are in this together. Like it or not, I'm coming with you.'

'What she said,' Jay added.

'Whatever you are doing, you had best do it now,' Hex warned and sure enough, the Gate began to falter and sputter.

Tobias looked from his friends to the closing Gate. If he really wanted to go, he didn't have time to argue.

'Fine,' he said at last and then leapt through.

Chapter 14

Ducking low and immediately scanning the area for danger, Tobias appeared on the other side of the Gate in a small dark chamber. It was a plain room with dull brown walls, a sandy floor, and four simple pillars holding up a low, domed roof. The gate behind him was nothing more than a frame of roughly carved stone, similar in size and shape to the cupboard doorway.

Scavenger was the next to come through, closely followed by Kayt and then Jay. Jay's feet had barely touched the floor when the Gate finally cut out in a soft shower of sand.

Tobias motioned for his friends to stay quiet and hide, then ducked in behind a wide stone pillar. Both Kayt and Jay did the same.

On the opposite side of the chamber, and standing in the centre, was a creature which looked like it could very well be the one he had seen before. The one that had escaped when Mr. Leach had arrived.

It reminded him of the goblins he had seen in books. Small and scrawny with a deep green skin. Its hunched posture meant that only the top of its head was visible over its stooped shoulders.

As Tobias watched, it stopped in its tracks and began sniffing loudly at the air. Panic set in immediately and fearing that it might spot them, he pressed himself tight in against the stone work.

The sniffing continued for a moment and then there was silence. Tobias dared a glance around the pillar. The creature was still there but now it was turning from side to side, examining its surroundings suspiciously. As it twisted around to look over its shoulder, its face came into view.

It wasn't pretty. In fact it was completely grotesque. Its eyes, while large, were also lidless, milky white, and bore no sign of pupils. It also had sharp pointed ears, two thin slits in place of a nose, and a mouth so wide it almost split the face in two. The whole head was encased in papery skin which looked like it had been stretched too tight over the skull.

The thing sniffed at the air again and the slits in the middle of its face flared outwards as it did. Tobias had no idea how good the creature's sense of smell was, but it obviously couldn't smell them because after giving a dismissive shrug, it shambled off through an archway and out of sight.

Jay emerged first. 'What was that?'

'A Porigast,' Hex replied. 'They are wretched, horrible little creatures. That one is probably one of Dvesh's servants.'

'Do you think it has the Key?' Tobias asked.

'That would make sense. It is probably here to let the Shadow Hunters in and out, but we still don't know what the key might be.'

'Should we go after it?'

'I can't believe I have to say this to you of all people, but don't rush in. We have to be careful.'

'Okay.' Tobias knew that Hex was right but he was also feeling very impatient. Considering that he had led his friends into this unknown world, he didn't want them to stay any longer than they had to.

'Let's follow it and see where it goes,' Kayt suggested.

They moved out from behind the pillars and made for the archway. There was a short corridor and on the other side of that was a bright white light.

Leading the way, Tobias emerged to find that the chamber was in fact little more than a compact, single story building of rough brown clay. There were no other rooms, and no larger structure. Just four crude walls and the slightly domed roof.

This realisation was only made more shocking by the fact that the land in which they now found themselves was a scorched and desolate world of endless, sun baked dirt and barren terrain. A fiery red sun dominated the sky and singed Tobias' eyes just as much as it did the earth. In the distance immense rock formations jutted sharply up from the ground and loomed over the land like angry stone tyrants.

Squinting hard against the harsh light, Tobias tried his best to find the Porigast, but the heat created a shimmering haze in the air which distorted everything more than a few feet away. He had to use his hand to shield his face just so he could open his eyes enough to make out any details at all.

Unfortunately, the Porigast did not seem to be affected by the sun in the way that Tobias did, and by the time he spotted it, shuffling around just a few feet away from the chamber entrance, It had already turned around to face them and was hissing angrily in their direction.

Tobias immediately raised Fear Bane, but it was too late. In the time it took Tobias to react, the creature had already begun to flee. It was moving with incredible speed and would be out of Tobias' sight long before he could do anything about it.

The Porigast was also screaming loudly as it ran, and these screams were soon answered by an ear piercing shriek which filled the air and froze Tobias in his tracks.

It was a baleful call, brimming with anger and malice. A sound which caused his muscles to tense and involuntarily flinch away from the threat. With the sound came a darkness which passed over, momentarily blocking out the sun and engulfing the ground in a deep shadow.

Tobias turned back to his friends and frantically began pushing them back into the safety of the chamber behind them. 'Get back!' he screamed at them before scanning the sky for the shadow's source.

What he saw was undoubtedly a bird, but it was unlike any bird from the mortal realm. It's size was so immense that even at a distance, Tobias could still make out the details of each feather which all glistened with a dark blue sheen. Its wings were spread wide, and tucked up beneath its body were two gnarled fleshy legs which ended in monstrously long grasping talons.

The bird shrieked again, and as it did, its beak parted to reveal a glistening red mouth. The Porigast did not look afraid however. Instead it was jumping up and down, screaming loudly and waving its thin arms as if trying to get the bird's attention. In response the bird tucked its massive wings into its side, stretched out its neck and began a steep dive straight in the direction of where Tobias was standing.

That was when Tobias realised that the Porigast was not afraid because this bird was on its side.

'You have to do something,' Hex yelled out, but Tobias couldn't move. The shrill screeches of the bird had locked up his muscles, and the sight of this huge beast hurtling towards him sent his mind into a panicked and feverish need to assign a name to the thing.

Blood Talon, Soaring Shadow, Nightmare Bird, Shrieking Death. His brain was tripping over countless words and ideas which swarmed up. It made no sense to become so consumed by such things in the presence of such immediate danger, but no matter how hard he tried to focus on the simple task of moving, his brain would not cooperate.

Closing the distance, the bird became a blur of movement which descended towards the ground at such speed Tobias was sure it would drive straight through. Then, when it was just a few metres away, its wings unfurled, its legs extended, and with a blast of air which battered everything in the area, it came to a sharp but stable landing.

Its feathers glinted in the sun like midnight blue pearls and it's beak, large enough to swallow Tobias whole, released a truly deafening caw.

Tobias looked up at it in both awe and terror. The colour of it's feathers alone would have made it a truly magnificent sight, but such wonder was lost in the terror of the situation. Not to mention the smell which emanated from the creature. It was a stale, fetid, coppery smell which made Tobias think of death.

'Tobias!' Kayt screamed from inside the Gate chamber.

It was just enough to snap Tobias into reality and he dived backwards mere moments before the brown clay walls around him erupted in a shower of jagged shards.

The bird drove down with its beak again, this time biting hard at a remnant of the wall and casting it aside like it was paper.

As the bird's beak beat down towards him, and the rancid stench filled the air, all Tobias could do was keep crawling backwards. He was frantically trying to keep some distance between himself and the razor edged beak.

More walls shattered and the bird struck the ground by Tobias' feet hard enough to leave a deep fracture in the floor.

He was running out of the corridor and was getting closer to the main chamber where he knew his friends were hiding. It suddenly occurred to him that if the bird destroyed the walls there, the roof could cave in on them. That realisation ignited a spark deep inside him which demanded action.

Tobias pushed hard with his feet, propelling himself backwards far enough that he had at least some solid wall left between him and the bird. At the same time, he whipped Fear Bane around to point in the direction of his attacker.

Even while laid on his back and surrounded by wreckage, Tobias felt the power course through his body and he summoned the orange mist around the blade. The feeling was so intoxicating that he even smiled slightly as he launched a torrent of swift attacks.

Streaks of orange sliced across the bird's chest and neck, exploding in fountains of energy and feathers, but to Tobias' dismay, they didn't appear to cause the bird anything beyond a slight annoyance.

It drove down again, this time biting at the air just inches away from Tobias' face. It would have been even closer but what remained of the passage was still tall enough to offer some protection.

The attack also opened the bird up to yet another strike from Fear Bane, but this time Tobias aimed straight at its head as the beak snapped and sliced at the air in front of him. Blood erupted from the side of the bird's face and it screeched in pain, rocketing backwards. It was not a killing blow but Tobias knew that his attack had finally found its mark and done some damage.

Feeling encouraged by the small victory, Tobias climbed to his feet and moved to press his advantage. The bird had staggered back and was waving its head around in a frenzy, spraying a long line of crimson fluid through the air.

Clambering over the rubble, Tobias launched another attack which caught it along the chest and sliced a number of feathers in half.

The bird did not risk further injury and as Tobias prepared to attack again, it propelled itself upwards with its powerful legs and beat its wings. Blasted by the sudden surge of wind, Tobias' attack was knocked off course. It sliced nothing but tail feathers as the bird escaped across the barren expanse that stretched out around them.

Tobias screamed in fury. Adrenaline was still coursing through his veins and the sensation of ecstasy that came with wielding Fear Bane was burning strong within him. Eager for a new target he spun on where he had last seen the Porigast, but the goblin creature was nowhere to be seen. All that remained was empty, arid wasteland, which stretched out in all directions.

A noise caught his attention behind him and he whirled around, bringing the point of Fear Bane up and ready to strike.

'Whoa there!' Jay yelled with his hands up as if surrendering.

Seeing his arm outstretched and the weapon pointing straight in the fear filled face of his friend, Tobias was instantly startled back into reality. In that moment, the horror of what he could have done caused his grip to loosen. Fear Bane dropped to the ground.

'I'm sorry,' Tobias said as he quickly scooped the weapon back up into its cloth bindings and pushed it into his bag.

'It's okay,' Jay replied, but he still looked more than a little shaken and he watched Tobias with obvious apprehension.

There was a moment of awkward stillness as the two boys stood staring at the ground, uncertain what to say to each other. Thankfully the tension was swiftly broken when Kayt emerged with Scavenger and Hex broke the silence.

'Did anyone see where the Porigast went?' He asked.

'I think he ran that way,' Kayt replied. She was pointing out across the desert to the distant rocky outcroppings.

'We need to find him,' Hex continued. 'He has the Key, and without that, we are never going to get out of here.'

Chapter 15

Shielding his eyes with the back of his hand, Jay squinted up at the sun. 'This is a disaster,' he grumbled.

They had set off in the direction they thought the Porigast had gone, but after two hours of walking, all they had discovered was more dry dirt and rocky earth. There wasn't any shelter or respite from the heat and the temperature only seemed to rise as they trudged forward across the desolate land.

Tobias could feel his skin prickling as it burned and sweat poured from every part of his body. It would have soaked his clothes if the heat didn't cause it to evaporate so quickly. There was no escape from the intense discomfort, but somehow, Tobias just couldn't find the energy to care. Everything had gone wrong, and no matter how far they walked, they would probably never get home.

He looked up at Jay who was now staring straight at him as if this was all his fault.

'Don't blame me,' Tobias snapped.

'I didn't blame you. But now you mention it, it was your idea to come to this place.'

'It wasn't my idea for you to come along. That was all you.'

'Sorry for wanting to help. I won't bother next time.'

'Who says I need your help. I can manage perfectly fine on my own. I did it last time.'

'Maybe you were just lucky last time,'

'Or maybe it is because I'm not a lumbering idiot.'

Jay stopped in his tracks and rounded on Tobias. 'Say that again,' His fists were clenched tight and his face flushed red.

In response Tobias straightened himself up so he was as tall as he could manage and locked eyes with Jay. His hands twitched, eager to reach for Fear Bane and end this argument.

'Do it!' The voice in the back of his mind purred in excited delight.

The two boys were moments away from coming to open blows when Kayt threw herself in between them. She put one hand on Jay's chest, and stared angrily between him and Tobias. Scavenger was tucked into her other arm.

'Pack it in you two,' she commanded them. 'I don't know what has gotten into you, but it is not helping anyone.'

Neither Tobias or Jay responded. Instead they just stared angrily at each other over Kayt's head. It was Hex who spoke.

'It is this place,' he explained. 'The corruption seeps into a person's soul and heightens despair, anger and irritability.'

'How do we snap them out of it?'

'Why bother? We are trapped, lost and probably never getting back to your world. You might as well just accept that we have already lost and just let them get on with it.'

'This is ridiculous,' Kayt said with a massive sigh of frustration. Then turning to face Tobias she slapped him hard across his cheek.

'Ow. What was that for?'

'To snap you out of this ridiculous mood. You and Hex are meant to be our guides here and you are both letting the place get to you. Pack it in or I swear, I will slap you silly.'

Jay grumbled and muttered something under his breath about Tobias deserving it, but Kayt rounded on him next and shot him a stern look.

'Don't think I won't knock some sense into you too,' she said.

In response, Jay went dutifully quiet and looked down at his feet.

Tobias lifted a hand and felt his face. It was tender and warm where Kayt had struck him, but it had worked. Although he could still feel the despair of Vikessa pressing down on him, he was no longer allowing it to seep in and turn him against his friends. Kayt was right. He and Hex should be taking the lead and protecting the others, not picking arguments.

Apparently content that she had restored some order, Kayt turned away from the two boys and began pacing backwards and forwards while looking at the ground.

'What are you doing?' Jay asked.

'Well, this is just a big desert isn't it. It just makes sense that if that thing had passed by recently, it would have disturbed the sand and left tracks. We just need to find them.'

Tobias watched Kayt as she continued searching the area. Jay shook his head as if baffled, but then also joined in the hunt. Even Scavenger began to hop backwards and forwards, sniffing at the earth every now and again.

'Well,' Hex said. 'What are you waiting for? The girl has a point. Get looking.'

Tobias did as he was told. He walked out in a different direction to Kayt and began scouring the ground for any sign of disturbance or tracks. A niggling feeling at the back of his mind told him that it was all pointless, and that they were going to be stuck here no matter what they did, but he fought it off. Kayt was right. Such thoughts would not help. They needed ideas which would.

'What are you doing?' Jay asked when he noticed that Tobias was not only searching for tracks, but also scooping up any loose stones that he found.

'I'm marking our trail,' Tobias replied. 'We need to be able to find our way back to the Gate, so I'm going to build little markers that we can follow.'

'That's a brilliant idea.' Kayt said.

'It's pretty good I suppose,' Jay added. He was clearly trying his best to sound unimpressed but he began picking up stones anyway.

'Has anyone found any…' Kayt began after several more minutes of looking, but she was sharply cut off by a loud squeak from Scavenger who was bouncing up and down excitedly.

All three of them rushed over to the little creature to see what he had found, but there didn't appear to be anything there. Just another dry patch of dirt. Despite this, Scavenger was looking at them with something resembling a proud, toothy smile, and as soon as he knew he had their attention, he pushed his nose to the ground and began following an invisible trail.

They all watched as Scavenger crawled in a straight line towards the closest of the rocky outcroppings, snorting and sneezing every so often to clear sand from his nostrils.

'I think he has picked up a scent,' Jay said.

'Looks like it,' Tobias replied.

'Should we follow him?'

'Probably.'

Despite his words, neither Tobias or Jay made any effort to move. Jay was slouched forward and staring blankly at the floor while Tobias' muscles felt heavy and weak. It was like he had been drained of all energy and he couldn't see much point in fighting it.

'Seriously!' Kayt took a big step forwards so that she could turn around and face them both. 'What is going on with you two?'

'I told you. It's this place,' Hex replied. 'I am honestly surprised that it doesn't seem to be affecting you.'

'I guess me and Scavenger are just better at being positive. I'm also more than happy to give you both a slap if you don't get moving.'

'Okay, okay,' Jay said, putting his hands up as if surrendering. 'I'm moving.'

'Yeah, me too,' Tobias added.

As they both began to slowly trudge along after Scavenger, Tobias heard Kayt muttering under her breath behind him.

'Bloody boys,' she said.

Chapter 16

Even with Scavenger's energy and Kayt pushing them on, Tobias still found the trek to be hard and slow. The huge monolith of jagged stone was looming ever closer, but the sun showed no sign that it was getting any lower in the sky. It was beating down on them with unforgiving heat, and the dryness of the air meant Tobias couldn't even produce saliva to keep his throat from becoming parched and sore.

He took a bottle of water out of his bag and had another gulp before handing it over to Jay.

'Thanks,' Jay said as he took the bottle and drained the last mouthful.

'I only have one more bottle,' Tobias told him.

'I guess there's not a lot we can do about it now. Hopefully we can reach the shadow of that thing before we collapse. At least we would die in the shade.' Though it sounded like Jay meant the last comment as a joke, his voice was a glum monotone with no hint of humour.

Despite this, Tobias followed where Jay was pointing and looked out at the outcropping. It did indeed cast a huge shadow across the land but Tobias doubted they could reach it before dehydration took them. But then again, maybe that was just the way this place was making him think. Maybe they could make it. He tried to stay positive.

In an attempt to take his mind off his thirst, Tobias turned his attention to what was ahead of him. Scavenger was still darting around on the ground, maintaining his lock on the scent trail. Behind him, Kayt was showing signs of slowing and her walk had become laboured, but she still kept up and held her head high. She only ever seemed to stop when she needed to grab a drink or place another pile of stones as a marker.

Beyond both Scavenger and Kayt, however, only one thing dominated Tobias' view, and that was the outcropping itself. Now they were closer, he could make out more details.

It was a gargantuan pillar of rough rock which thrust up like a vicious spike desperately trying to impale the sky. If there had been any clouds, it would have easily been tall enough to pierce above them. Despite the sharpness of the point, however, the base was far from narrow. The structure tapered as it rose, with ragged spikes jutting off at various intervals.

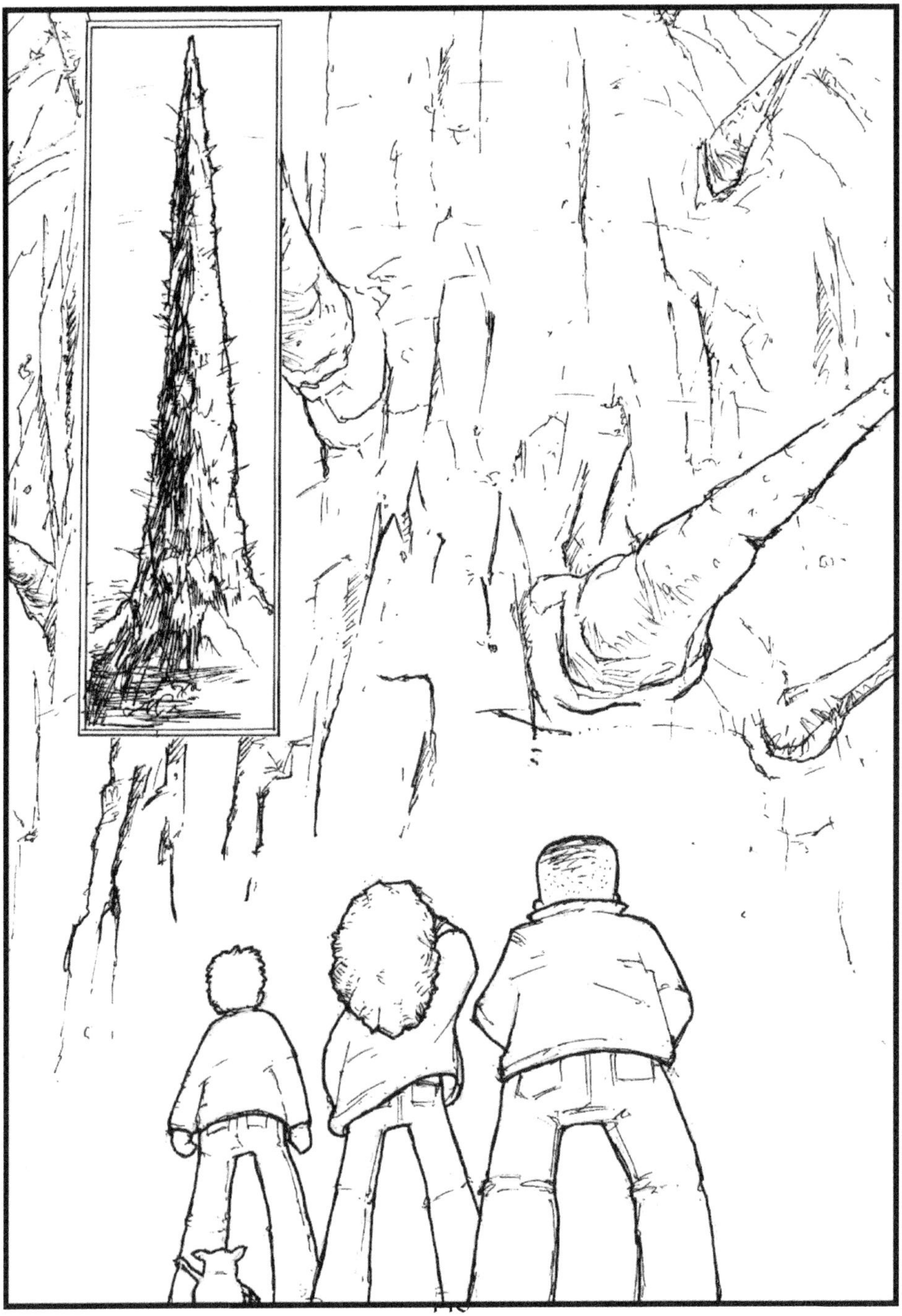

The closer they got to the structure, the more it became clear just how wide it was. By the time they reached the edge of its shadow, and the truly immense scale of the thing became clear, Tobias suspected that it would take a good few hours just to walk around its base.

'I think Scavenger is getting tired,' Hex said as they stepped into the relative cool of the shadow. It was still very warm but without the constant blaze of the sun, it didn't feel quite so oppressive. There was also a slight breeze, which while carrying a stale, damp scent, was also welcome.

'We must have been going for a couple of hours by now,' Jay added. 'Maybe he needs a break.'

Tobias looked at Scavenger. His friend had definitely slowed down but he didn't look tired. He was still hopping around with as much energy as ever, but he was sniffing at the air in all different directions and bouncing backwards and forwards in a way which meant he was covering the same ground over and over again.

'He isn't tired,' Tobias replied. 'I think he has lost the scent.'

'Oh, great. That's all we need,' Jay began, but when Kayt shot him an angry look he went quiet.

'It's not his fault,' she said as she kneeled down and patted Scavenger gently on the head. 'It will be this wind. It smells like the back of my dad's washing machine. It's probably covering up the smell of the Porigast.

'So what do we do?' Jay asked.

Kayt pointed over at the pillar of dark rock. 'The Porigast was clearly heading towards that thing. Maybe we should just keep going in that direction.'

Jay shrugged. 'That is still a hell of a walk though. And if we are going in the wrong direction, we will have lost it completely.'

'It's all I have. Unless you have any better ideas.'

'You know I don't.'

'Exactly, My Dad always says, if you ever have a hard decision to make, it is better to push on with the wrong decision than waste time with no decision. He also…'

'Your Dad doesn't half say a lot of rubbish,' Jay interrupted. The irritation was clear in his voice. 'He must whitter on almost as much as you.'

Kayt planted her hands on her hips and peered over her glasses to lock eyes with Jay. 'I know that is just this place making you say that, so I'm just going to ignore it.'

'Do what you want. I think I preferred it when you used to avoid me.'

'Well that was before I found out you could be a decent human being. It is a shame that didn't last long though.'

'Whatever.' Jay gave a dismissive wave of his hand. 'Anyway, I still don't think we should just wander off blindly. Especially if it takes us further away from that Gate thing.'

'Of course you don't. You would prefer to just curl up here and give in wouldn't you. Well I won't let that happen.'

'You really think you can stop me do you?'

'As it happens, I do.'

'Go on then, give it your best shot.'

Tobias watched the argument unfold. At first he didn't have the energy to become involved, but the more the two squared up to each other, the more he could see just how ragged they had become.

Jay was definitely the worst. He wasn't drawing himself up to his full height like he usually did, and his arms were hanging limply by his side. Even his eyelids looked heavy and drooped down in a way which made him look half asleep.

Kayt was also looking weaker, her freckled cheeks were red with sunburn, her hair frizzy and dry, and her body slumped in a way that betrayed just how much of her energy was being forced.

'Let's just take a rest for a moment,' Tobias said at last. They all clearly needed it, and there was no point making any decisions when they were all so on edge.

'Could you find us some shelter?' Tobias asked Scavenger and in response, the little creature squeaked, sniffed the air again, and then scuttled off in the direction of the breeze.

'Do you really think rest is a good idea?' Hex asked. 'We shouldn't be staying in this place any longer than we have to.'

'I know. But we can't keep pushing ourselves. We need to regain some energy if we are to keep our heads straight. Otherwise, we will just end up turning on each other.'

'Okay, but let's keep the rest short.'

Tobias nodded, but before anyone could say anything else, Scavenger re-appeared a short distance away and chirped loudly to get their attention.

'Looks like he has found something,' Kayt said with a smile. 'He really is so awesome.'

'He really is,' Tobias replied, and they all began making their way in that direction.

Chapter 17

After catching up with Scavenger, the small rodent led them along the edge of the shadow before cutting inwards slightly towards the outcropping. It was only a few minutes of fast paced walking but they eventually came to a patch of rocky earth which rose from the sand in a low ridge before dropping back down into a large bowl shape.

The dip was easily big enough for them all to sit in, and it was indeed sheltered from both the breeze and the sand. As Tobias slid down into the depression, he also noticed that it was much cooler, with droplets of condensation forming on the stone.

'This is perfect,' Kayt said once they were all settled.

'You did a good job,' Tobias told Scavenger before pulling some biscuits out of his bag and handing him one.

Tobias looked up at the other two. They were also pulling food out of their bags and trying to get comfortable.

'We won't stay here long,' Tobias told them. 'Just enough to get a bit of energy and work out what to do next.'

Both Jay and Kayt nodded.

'So is this how you remember it?' Kayt asked around a mouthful of crisps.

'This is nothing like the Underlands,' Tobias replied. 'This feels like an actual world. The Underlands was more of a dungeon maze.'

'So is this place worse?'

Tobias thought about the question for a moment. Vikessa did have the endless dry desert and unforgiving sun to contend with. And he had felt a constant sensation of hopelessness and frustration while he had been there. But then thoughts of the Underlands brought back memories of genuine terror and torments. Far beyond the scope of anything he could have possibly imagined. Every second in the Underlands had been a battle for survival against un-natural horrors and his own crippling fear. In comparison Vikessa felt more like Terrascura.

'It's hard to say,' he admitted at last. 'The Underlands feel like they were much worse, but I was a very different person then.'

'Can we not talk about this please?' Jay asked. He was still not looking great. Despite pushing a piece of chocolate into his mouth, he did not look like he was enjoying it. His chewing looked like it was a chore, and his whole body still sagged as if all the fight had been sapped out of him. Despite this, his eyes darted from side to side with a nervous energy and his voice still held a biting tone.

'Sorry,' Tobias replied. 'How are you feeling.'

'How do you think I am feeling?' Jay snapped. 'This place is hot and horrible, and we are stuck here. We are probably going to die in this hole with no way home.'

Tobias put down his biscuits and leaned in to place a hand on Jay's shoulder. 'I promise, I will do everything I can to get us home. We just have to hold onto what little hope we have and not let this place win.'

'I guess,' Jay said. Then, after a moment's silence, he added, 'I'm sorry for calling you wimp before. You are definitely tougher than you look.'

'It's okay,' Tobias replied with a smile. 'You aren't as bad as I thought either.'

'Hey,' Kayt interrupted, trying to look stern but barely suppressing a grin. 'I hope you are also sorry for calling me Freako?'

Despite himself, the corners of Jay's lips twitched into a slight smile of his own. 'I guess. I mean, you are still kind of odd, but it's a good kind of odd. Know what I mean?'

'So it's a compliment?'

'I suppose.'

'I'll take that.'

The three of them laughed. It was only a small laugh which trailed off quickly, but it felt good all the same. Even Jay looked a little happier as he swallowed another piece of chocolate.

Jay shoved the last of his bar into his mouth and then looked back up at Tobias. 'I heard that your parents are dead,' he said in an incredibly casual tone.

'Jay!' Kayt looked horrified but Jay just seemed confused by her obvious shock at his statement.

'What? My parents are dead too. It's no big deal.'

'How did they die?' Tobias asked. It hadn't occurred to him that his friends might have also lost their parents.

'My mum died when I was born. I'm actually just assuming my dad is dead because I don't have a clue who he was. I live with my gran now.'

'I never met my mum either,' Kayt said. 'Dad says she moved away for work.'

'What does she do?'

'I don't know. My dad used to say she was a princess but that seems unlikely. I think he was just saying it because I was so young. He hasn't spoken much about her for years now.'

'I guess we are all missing parents then,' Jay said. There was a hint of sadness to his voice, but Tobias could think of nothing to say and simply nodded.

Kayt shifted slightly and turned to face the purple gem which hung around Tobias' neck. 'What about you, Hex?' She asked. 'What were your parents like?'

'My mother was a Clonithedair and my father was a powerful Lord. He ruled a portion of the Underlands called Preat Spinam.'

'What is a Clonithedair?'

'I suppose it is kind of like a priestess to the Witch Mother. They are fanatical followers who aspire to prove themselves worthy to her. It was because of this devotion that my parents gave me as a gift to the Witch Mother when I was just a child. I haven't seen them since, but it is my great desire that they are indeed dead. I hate them for handing me over to that monster, but I would not like to have to kill them myself.'

The three children sat staring at the stone in stunned silence before Jay eventually broke the tension by saying 'Woah, that is intense.'

'It is what it is,' Hex replied. 'It's not like Tobias is ever getting me out of this stone anyway.'

'Let's not get into any more arguments,' Kayt said, quickly cutting Tobias off as he opened his mouth to reply. 'How about we think about what to do next?'

Jay looked up with a shrug. 'What's the point? That creature could be anywhere by now.'

'The point is to not give up hope. We know it was heading in this direction, and since the mountain is the only thing here, it was probably heading to that.'

Kayt's right,' Tobias said. 'We need to keep positive. If we let this place get to us, then we really have lost.'

Jay idly picked up a small black pebble and flicked it through the air. It hit the edge of the rocks with a soft click before rattling back down the slope and coming to a rest at the bottom.

'Okay,' he said with a heavy sigh. 'What do we do?'

Tobias pulled Hex from around his neck and laid him in the middle of where they were all sitting.

'What do you know about this place?' He asked the stone.

'I've only been to Vikessa once,' Hex replied. 'But I never saw the outside of Dvesh's castle.'

'Did you meet Dvesh?'

'No. I was just getting books from his library for the Witch Mother. The Masters cannot cross Gate's themselves. They are prisoners in their own realms. They communicate with each other using magical artifacts, and rely on lesser beings, like myself, to perform any tasks which require travelling between the realms.'

'What was the castle like?' Kayt asked.

'To be honest, I thought it was a little bit gaudy. Dvesh enjoys displaying his wealth and there wasn't a room or corridor that wasn't heavily decorated with precious metals or silks. It was also disconcerting how many Subservients he kept.'

'Subservients?'

'Mortal slaves. All the Masters have them to perform menial chores, but Dvesh surrounds himself with them just so he can entertain himself by tormenting and torturing them. The castle has several dungeons built for just that purpose.'

Kayt gave an audible gasp. 'That's horrible.'

'Cruelty is not uncommon in the Realms, though it is no secret that Dvesh is a particularly malicious creature, even in comparison to the other Masters. He is the weakest of their number and I think he torments lesser beings as a way to make himself feel better about his position.'

'I'm sorry, but how is any of this going to help us?' Jay asked irritably.

'I don't know,' Kayt replied. 'But it never hurts to know your enemy.'

'Okay, so we know this guy likes to hurt people and that he is a bit of a bully. That still doesn't tell us where to go.'

'He is more than a bit of a bully,' Hex snapped. 'He is a black hearted creature of pure evil and immense cunning. Do not mistake him for a petty ruffian.'

'It still doesn't…' Jay didn't finish the sentence before his eyes suddenly widened and his mouth fell slack. He wasn't looking at Hex anymore, nor was he looking at Tobias. Instead he seemed completely focused on something behind them.

'What is it?' Tobias asked. He didn't dare turn around himself.

'I have no idea,' Jay whispered. 'But I'm pretty sure it is going to kill us.

Chapter 18

Tobias kept his eyes fixed on Jay while carefully reaching out for his bag. The other boy's face had drained of all colour and he was beginning to slowly crawl backwards, away from whatever it was which had now appeared at the edge of the ridge behind Tobias' back. Both Kayt and Scavenger were also now staring up out of the ditch and they too were keeping low while shifting backwards.

As if in response to this movement, the thing behind Tobias began to emit a loud series of clicking and scratching noises which conjured images of a giant insect or spider, scuttling along the floor and chirping through large vicious mandibles. Tobias knew his imagination was working feverishly to create the most grotesque image that it could manage, but he also knew that this thing was bad enough to terrify Jay. Not wanting his mind to get the better of him, Tobias gave his bag one last tug towards him and reached inside.

A blast of energy surged up Tobias' arm as his hand grasped around the warm handle of Fear Bane. He could feel the power take hold as it caused his muscles to tense and his mind to focus. With the weapon in hand, he spun around and thrust it forward.

'Do it!' the voice in his head screamed. 'Destroy it!'

Tobias drew fear into the blade of Fear Bane and manifested it as the thick orange smoke which gathered and coiled around his hand. There was a lot of it. More than he had ever seen before. It was so dense that he couldn't even see a glint of Fear Bane's metal beneath the churning mass.

Some of the fear was from him, some from Kayt, and a slightly larger mass ebbed from Jay. But there was still more. More tendrils coiling in with the others, adding to the power and flooding Tobias with an even greater sense of strength.

'Kill it,' the voice hissed angrily. 'Kill it now!'

Tobias tried to ignore it, but it seemed closer than usual. Like it had a firmer grasp on his mind. He clenched his eyes tight and forced it back. The presence did not fade easily and the effort was almost painful.

Eventually, Tobias regained control, and opening his eyes, he could immediately see that the extra fear was actually coming from the creature. It wasn't angry or aggressive. It was terrified.

Tobias lowered Fear Bane and released the energy harmlessly to disperse into the air.

'What are you doing?' Jay asked, but Tobias was already tuning him out. Instead, he walked up the bank and towards the creature in front of him.

It was gigantic. Easily the size of a bus. And while it did have a vague insectoid appearance, it also had elements which looked almost plant like. Its body was covered with a black insect-like shell and its six long spindly legs resembled those of a cockroach. Even its head looked like that of a bug with a row of round black eyes glinting in the shadowy light.

Contrasting sharply with the dull colour of its body, however, were two purple stalks which grew from atop its head like antennae, but which ended in strange purple flower heads. From two arms also sprouted what looked like enormous purple petals, and from within these petals emerged long blue vines which twitched and probed at the air.

The thing would have looked like a truly horrific beast if it wasn't for the fact that Tobias could physically see the sheer amount of fear which was radiating from its body. It enshrouded the creature like a cloak formed entirely out of orange mist.

'It's scared,' Tobias shouted back to his friends.

'I don't care,' Jay replied. 'It's huge and it will probably eat us. Kill it!'

Tobias looked up at the unblinking black eyes and blue vines, which were now drawing back into the enclosing petals.

'I don't think it wants to hurt us,' he said.

'Of course it wants to hurt us. It's a monster.'

'Actually, I think we surprised it by being here. It probably just came here for the moisture.'

Pushing Fear Bane back into his bag, Tobias pulled his sleeve down till it covered his hand and rubbed it on the damp rock beside him. He then stepped forward, and with a silent prayer that he was right, held it out towards the creature.

'Careful,' Kayt called out behind him, but it was already too late.

The creature edged closer and one of its long pointed legs stepped into the ditch a few feet away from Tobias. It clicked loudly as it connected with the hard rock. Using the leg to support itself, the thing leaned down and regarded Tobias for a moment. Then one of the petal clusters at the ends of its arms parted and the vines emerged once again.

Each one of the petals was as large as Tobias himself and the vines were long enough that they could easily wrap around him a dozen times over, but he resisted the urge to flinch back as one snaked towards his arm.

In a juddery, tentative motion, the vine slowly reached the wet sleeve, and with a gentle prod, it tested for danger. Apparently happy that there was no threat, the vine moved with more surety as it began wrapping its way around Tobias' arm and absorbed the water. It was an odd sensation with a gentle pressure and a coolness where the damp sleeve was sucked dry.

Tobias looked back over his shoulder at the horrified faces of Jay and Kayt. 'See. It just wants a drink.'

Scavenger hopped a little closer but remained safely tucked behind Tobias leg. The creature was immense compared to Tobias so he could only imagine what it must have looked like to something as small as Scavenger.

'I'm not sure you could pass this one off as a pet,' Hex said from around Tobias' neck.

'Probably not, but it would be fun to see my uncle's reaction if I brought it home.' Tobias laughed and the sudden sound seemed to startle the creature. The vine retracted sharply into the petals and it scuttled backwards.

'I'm sorry,' Tobias said, but it was too late. The spooked creature turned and darted off across the desert towards the rocky spire.

'Do you know what that was?' Tobias asked Hex.

'Presumably something native to Vikessa, but beyond that, I am afraid I have no idea.'

'I'm going to call it a Skitter.'

'As good a name as any I suppose.'

'I think we should follow it,' Tobias added as he turned around to face the others.

Jay looked aghast at the idea. 'Why on earth would we do that?'

'I don't know. I just feel like it's the right way to go.'

'Well we haven't come up with any better ideas,' Kayt replied and she immediately began bundling stuff back into her backpack.

Chapter 19

It was impossible to keep pace with the Skitter. Even if they hadn't had to gather their things and clamber up the bank of the rocky ditch, the thing moved with incredible speed. It would have left them behind regardless of how quickly they got ready.

Thankfully, it was not hard to track. The six pointed legs left clear marks in the soft sand, and it was heading in a straight line towards the spire.

'How did you know it wasn't dangerous?' Kayt asked Tobias as they walked.

'I didn't know for certain, but it hadn't attacked us and I knew it was frightened.'

'Because you can see fear?'

'Yeah. The Skitter was covered in it.'

'That is awesome. You are like a superhero.'

'I don't know about that.' Tobias looked down at the hard ground in an effort not to make eye contact. 'To be honest, my powers actually scare me. Fear is not a good emotion and I am always worried that I will lose control.' He chose not to mention the dark presence which also existed at the back of his mind.

'But it doesn't have to be a bad emotion,' Kayt said as she placed a hand on Tobias' shoulder. 'People don't like being afraid, but sometimes it keeps you safe. And in this case, your powers stopped a fight which would have resulted in someone getting hurt.'

'I guess. I hadn't really thought about it like that.'

'Like my dad says, every negative can be a positive if given a chance.'

Tobias looked up and smiled at Kayt. He couldn't help but wonder if her dad really did say all these things, but hearing them did help.

'Thanks Kayt.'

'Anytime bestie.'

After that, the group continued following the tracks in silence. Jay was once again looking particularly glum, dragging his feet and walking with a slump to his posture. Tobias also felt the weight of hopelessness pushing in. Whenever it began to get him down, however, he just looked over to Scavenger cheerfully bounding along and let the sight bring a smile to his lips.

After another several minutes, they finally reached the edge of the rocky spire. It towered above them now and Tobias had to crane his neck to follow the line of it into the air. Even then, he could no longer see the peak.

Up ahead, jutting out from the base of the spire was a large pile of fallen rubble and boulders which formed a crude but impassable wall in their path. The Skitter tracks ran up to this obstacle before skirting along the edge and disappearing around the corner where the boulders ended.

'What is that noise?' Kayt asked.

Tobias stopped and listened. It was a faint sound which carried on the air and bounced off the rocks. Straining his ears, Tobias leaned forward and closed his eyes so that he could focus. It sounded like the clicking and chirping of the Skitter, but faster and more frantic. It was also accompanied by a number of small yelps and high pitched chatter.

Keeping low and trying not to make a sound themselves, Tobias led the way carefully towards the source of the noise. Scavenger was at his heel, and both Jay and Kayt were close behind. As they rounded the corner of the boulders, and there was no longer anything in the way to muffle the sound, it immediately went from a distant echo to a cacophonous din.

The clicking was indeed the Skitter, but rather than the cautious chittering of before, this was the panicked noise of pain and fear. The cause of this suffering was eight Porigasts, much like the one Tobias had seen when he had first entered Vikessa. These ones wore ragged leather vests and held weapons made from wood and sharpened bone. They appeared to have pinned the Skitter, blocking it from reaching a nearby cave, and they were jabbing at it while laughing and screeching at each other in wild delight.

It was a strange sight to see something so big and intimidating cowering away from a pack of creatures. Especially ones so tiny in comparison that it could easily swallow them whole. Yet there it was, the massive Skitter huddled up against the rockface and chittering desperately as the Porigasts assaulted it with spears and knives. The Skitter kept pulling its body against the wall and desperately trying to lift its legs out of harm's way, but everytime one leg pulled back, another had to go back down to maintain balance and the Porigasts would rush in to stab at it with excited glee.

'That poor thing,' Kayt exclaimed as soon as she rounded the corner and witnessed the attack.

'This is not our fight,' Hex whispered.

'I've got to agree with the rock on this one,' Jay added.

Kayt gave Tobias a pained look. 'It isn't even trying to defend itself. We should help it.'

Tobias couldn't help but agree with Kayt. He hated the idea of something suffering, especially as the result of bullies, and despite its appearance, the Skitter was clearly too terrified to retaliate. He was about to respond but Hex cut him off, almost as if anticipating Tobias' response.

'There is no way helping that thing could benefit us,' Hex insisted. 'It only puts us at unnecessary risk. Leave it and let nature take its course.'

'I can't do that,' Tobias replied. He swung his bag off his shoulder and withdrew Fear Bane. Instantly everything around him became sharper and more vivid, and the orange energy became visible. There was a soft glow around Tobias and his friends, but the Skitter was once again radiating fear like a beacon. Tobias could feel the force of it despite the distance.

'You can stay and hide here if you want,' he said to the others, 'but I'm going to help.'

'This is crazy,' Jay replied, showing no signs of moving.

Kayt, however, immediately started picking up small rocks and tossing them up and down in her hand, checking how good they were for throwing. 'I'll help anyway I can,' she said.

Scavenger also hopped forward and stood by Tobias' leg. He tried to raise his hackles and growl, but with no hair and a high pitched squeak, he didn't look anywhere near as intimidating as he obviously thought he did.

Jay watched all this with a stubborn grimace on his face, but when Kayt finished gathering her stones and stepped in beside Tobias, he huffed loudly and shrugged his shoulders. 'Well if Kayt's going, I'm not staying here alone. Besides, you will need some muscle.'

'Just stay behind me,' Tobias told all of them. Then taking one last deep breath, he stepped around the rubble and advanced on the Porigasts.

The Skitter was the first to notice the arrival of the three children and their strange pet. As it did, Tobias saw its fear spike even further. It clearly believed that they were there to join in the torment, but Tobias quickly proved their true intent by making the first attack.

He concentrated on Fear Bane, summoning up his own fears and anger to conjure the orange mist around the weapon. He didn't release this energy however. Instead he used it to reach out and take control of the churning torrent of fear which surrounded the Skitter.

He wove long strands of the energy into thick cords which he then gave form and brought into being. The sheer amount of the fear made the task much easier, and as it solidified, the normally smokey energy became a much more tangible, solid mass. They looked like fleshy orange tentacles rather than smokey tendrils, and Tobias could feel the force which was building up within them.

One of the tentacles emerged as if from the Skitter's back and lashed out at a nearby Porigast. The creature yelped in shock and pain as it was struck hard, sending it and its now shattered spear hurtling through the air. Another tentacle swung into the crowd of panicking monsters, and while most managed to avoid it, one of their number was not so lucky. The tentacle collided into its chest, swept it through the air and smashed it against the rock wall with a sickening crack.

Tobias grinned in delight. The control he was feeling was like a rush of adrenaline. It made him feel better than he had ever done in his life. He knew nothing could stop him while he wielded this power. He was a god.

One of the Porigasts darted back away from the swinging tentacles, and as it stumbled clear, it caught sight of Tobias and his friends. There was a shrill shriek and soon, all six of the remaining creatures were running in their direction.

'Looks like they have spotted us,' Hex said with a dry tone.

'Take that,' Kayt yelled as she hurled the first of her stones. It landed short, hitting the ground just in front of the first Porigast with a loud clatter. Her second stone found its mark though and struck the creature in the shoulder, causing it to trip before righting itself.

Following her lead, Jay also began hurling stones. His were bigger and flew with more strength but seemed far less accurate. Every time he missed, he got angrier and put even more power into the next throw. This resulted in yet another miss which only fueled the rage. By the time the Porigasts had closed some of the distance, Jay had all but given up throwing the stones and was looking for a larger rock to use as a weapon.

Scavenger was also waiting for the Porigasts to get close, and despite bouncing up and down in an effort to look scary, he clearly wasn't certain what to do next. Instead he kept close behind Tobias and offered the occasional squeak of encouragement.

Tobias was only dimly aware of what his friends were doing, however. He was entirely focused on the Porigasts and the power at his command. They were out of range of the tentacles now, so Tobias let them fade and instead began using the energy swirling around Fear Bane.

Forming thin shards, he launched them one after another at the oncoming creatures. One after another, the thin orange blades whipped through the air and sliced towards the Porigasts. The creatures were fast and nimble, their thin bony bodies dodging in an effort to avoid the attacks. Many of Tobias' attempts whistled by, or imbedded themselves into the dry earth, but still some found their mark.

One shard struck a Porigast across the face, cutting through its milky white eye and sending it spinning to the floor. Another sliced an arm of a second Porigast, causing it to lose its weapon and recoil in pain. Yet another cut into its leg as the Porigast clutched its bleeding shoulder and dropped it to the ground. By the time they were close enough to fight back, only four of the creatures remained.

Kayt screamed as one of them lunged at her with its spear but it was quickly knocked off its feet by a diving tackle from Jay who then struck it hard across the head with a large jagged rock.

Grabbing the creature's weapon, Jay stood back up and planted himself between Kayt and the rest of their attackers. He jabbed the spear at any who moved close.

Suddenly realising that they had lost more than half their number, the three remaining Porigasts became even more frenzied. They shrieked and chattered to each other in a language Tobias didn't understand.

'What are they saying?' he asked Hex.

'I don't know,' the stone replied.

Then a large black shape swooped through the air overhead.

Chapter 20

'Run!' Tobias screamed to his friends.

Jay thrust his spear out at the closest Porigast, forcing it to take another step back. Then grabbing Kayt by the arm, he dragged her over to the pile of rubble and ducked down against the rocks. Scavenger followed close behind but stopped when he noticed Tobias wasn't moving.

'Go!' Tobias ordered him, but the small rodent didn't listen. Instead, Scavenger rushed back to Tobias' leg and began pulling on his trousers in a desperate attempt to make him follow.

Tobias pushed Scavenger away with his foot. 'I got this,' he said. 'You go and hide.'

'Are you sure you know what you are doing?' Hex asked. 'Maybe we should run too.'

'I said I've got this!' Tobias yelled angrily. The orange energy around Fear Bane flared as he spoke and Scavenger was momentarily taken aback by the fury. He squeaked softly before hopping away and jumping into Kayt's arms.

Tobias turned his attention back to the Porigasts and the looming shape in the sky. He channelled all of his fear and anger into Fear Bane and dug his feet into the ground.

He had control. He had power. He wasn't going to let the Nightmare Bird get away this time.

Two more blasts of orange erupted from Fear Bane. One caught a Porigast hard across the chest, while the other cut into the leg of another. Both hit the floor with cries of pain.

Tobias spun to face the final Porigast and was about to send a shard at its head when he was thrown off balance by a powerful gust of warm air.

He caught himself before he fell and turned to face the massive bird as it came to land with its head looming over him. A shrill shriek echoed off the surrounding rocks and pierced at Tobias' ears but he did not lose concentration.

He fired blast after blast at the creature. Few penetrated the silky blue feathers, but the torrent kept it mercifully on the defensive and prevented it from pressing in. Tobias was building his power and looking for a weak spot. He was certain that he was going to win. He just needed an opening.

Another shard sliced through the feathers on the Nightmare Bird's neck and for a brief instant, as the creature reared back,

Tobias was sure he saw bare skin. He smiled, but before he could follow up on his attack, a sharp heat shot through his back.

Flinching away from the pain, he turned to see a Porigast drawing back a long blade, wet with blood. In the chaos of the battle, Tobias had not noticed the creature creeping up behind him, and as it raised the blade for another strike, there was no time to react.

In that instant, Tobias realised that this vile little creature was about to end his life, and despite all the power at his command, there was nothing he could do about it.

He watched the weapon lunge towards his chest as if it was moving in slow motion, but it never connected. In the same instant that the Porigast attacked, a spear whistled through the air and struck it in the neck. It hit the floor with a gurgling cry.

Tobias glanced over to the rocks and saw Jay stood over Kayt, his arm extended but his hand now empty. He owed the other boy his life.

There was no time to dwell on such things, however. The Nightmare Bird still remained and the fight was not over.

Turning back just in time to see the glistening beak of the beast bearing down on him, Tobias slashed at the air with Fear

Bane and released a razor sharp arc of energy which radiated out. Empowered by the fear Tobias had just felt, it struck deep into the creature's neck, bit deep, and erupted from the other side in a shower of feathers and crimson liquid.

As the last of the life drained from the twitching body of the Nightmare Bird and the dust settled, Tobias became aware of a new figure watching from atop the pile of rubble behind him. This newcomer was silently watching, and though it made no move to approach, it did not look friendly.

Its entire body was crooked and malformed, with a hunched back, gnarled limbs, and an oily black skin. Even its head was unnaturally long with two tiny eyes, a sharp nose and a twisted grin.

It began a slow clap.

Chapter 21

'Impressive,' the figure said with a high raspy voice, like sandpaper on glass. 'It is a true honour to be in the presence of the mighty Tyringar.'

'Who are you?' Tobias demanded as he turned Fear Bane to point straight at the newcomer.

There was a definite flash of worry on the figure's misshapen face, and for a single brief moment, Tobias saw the orange energy of fear flare around him.

'I mean you no harm, my lord Tyringar. I am merely a pathetic wretch who could never hope to match your dark splendour.'

The figure did look pathetic as it stood there, hunched over, rubbing its hands together and keeping its beady eyes on the floor just in front of Tobias' feet rather than actually making eye contact.

'Who are you?' Tobias asked again.

The figure entered a low bow which, due to his crooked spine, looked deeply uncomfortable.

'I am Dvesh,' he said. 'Your humble servant.'

'Be careful,' Hex whispered.

'Be careful?' Dvesh's rasping voice rose as if deeply offended. 'Why must he be careful? I mean him no harm. I wish only to aid the mighty Tyringar in his glorious endeavours.'

'I am not Tyringar,' said Tobias.

'Apologies my lord, but I must disagree. The Witch Mother would not be so worried if you were not indeed the Lord of Nightmares.'

'I am not Tyringar!' Tobias insisted again. 'My name is Tobias. Tobias Crow.'

'Well then Lord Crow, it is my honour to welcome you to my paltry little realm.'

'What is this game, Dvesh,' asked Hex, his temper hot and the impatience clear in his voice.

'Game? There is no game. I merely wish to offer my services.'

'Quit the act. We know you serve the Witch Mother, and that you sent the Shadow Hunter after Tobias.'

Dvesh held his deformed hands out in front of him as if surrendering. 'Okay, okay. I admit, I did send my pet, but it was not at the behest of the Witch Mother, but to bring you to me. I only wish to talk.'

'If you only wanted to talk, why not meet me when I came through the Gate? Why allow me to be attacked?'

'Apologies Lord Crow, I just had to be certain that you were who I believed you to be. I meant no offence. Please forgive this humble wretch.' Dvesh bowed low again.

Tobias was far from convinced, but Dvesh was showing no signs of a threat. If even a fraction of what he was saying was true, then maybe he really did want to speak.

'What do you want then?'

'I have an offer. A deal if you will.'

'What deal?' Hex asked.

'A deal that benefits us both greatly. A deal that protects us both and gives each of us what it is we desire.'

'Just get on with it,' Hex spat.

'Very well. But first a sign of good faith.'

Dvesh looked back over his shoulder and motioned with his hand for something to approach. As he did, a Porigast clambered up to the top of the rock pile next to him before sliding down the opposite side, towards Tobias.

Seeing the creature coming in their direction, Jay and Kayt quickly jumped out from their hiding spot and rushed over behind Tobias.

The Porigast was not alone either. As its feet hit the ground at the foot of the rocks, a pack of five Shadow Hunters also emerged at Dvesh's side. Ulike the Porigast, they did not make a move to approach. They just crouched low and watched with narrow, predatory eyes, their tails swishing through the air behind them.

Tobias took a small step backwards and held out an arm to shield his friends as the Porigast shuffled closer. Fear Bane was still brimming with energy and ready to attack but the Porigast showed no sign that it was worried. As it reached Tobias, it bent down to place something at his feet. A circle of polished silver metal glinted in the sand. Slightly reflective and perfectly smooth, it looked just large enough to wrap around a person's head like a crown.

'What is this?' Hex asked.

'This is what you seek,' Dvesh replied. His lips curled up at the edges. 'It is the Key back to your realm. A gift.'

Tobias looked down at the silver ring and back at the grotesque creature at the top of the rocks. 'I don't understand.'

'It really is very simple, my lord. If you agree to stay and talk with me for a while, I will allow your companions to take the Key and return home. Refuse and my pets will rip you all limb from limb.'

Tobias bent down and picked up the Key. He didn't take his eyes off the danger lurking at the top of the rise, but he was beginning to wonder if even more enemies lurked out of sight. With Fear Bane in his hand and the sense of power still hot in his mind, he was certain he had the power to destroy these five Shadow Hunters. Unfortunately he had no idea how powerful Dvesh was, and if there were enemies lurking out of sight, his friends would be in danger.

He spun around and pushed the Key into Kayt's hand.

'Go,' he said as he unlooped Hex from around his neck and hung him around hers.

'We can't leave you,' Kayt protested.

'You have to. You need to take Hex and Scavenger and get home. I will follow as soon as I can.'

Kayt dropped the silver circlet on the ground and planted her hands on her hips. 'I'm not going.'

Tobias leaned in and put his hands on her shoulders so that he was looking straight into her eyes. Tears were forming in the corners and beginning to form streaks down her freckled cheeks.

'You have to go,' he said. 'I will be right behind you.' Then turning to Jay, he added 'Make sure she is safe. Don't look back.'

Jay nodded, picked up the Key and grabbed Kayt's arm.

'Come on,' He said as forcefully as he could manage. 'Tobias will be fine.'

'I need you to make sure they get back safely,' Tobias told Scavenger. The small rodent squeaked in reply before snuggling into Tobias leg. After a quick pat, Scavenger then turned back to the others and began bounding along ahead, occasionally stopping and squeaking for them to follow.

'Good luck,' Jay said before pulling Kayt away.

'I will see you soon,' Hex added.

And then they were off. Running across the shadow cast earth towards the open light of the sun and the Gate which would get them home.

Tobias watched them for a moment to make sure that nothing was following or waiting to attack. Then he turned back to Dvesh. He was suddenly very aware that he was alone.

'Well that was almost heartwarming,' Dvesh said.

'If anything happens to them, I will kill you.' Tobias warned.

'Do not fear, my lord. The Key will get them home safely and nothing will block their way.'

Tobias stared at the misshapen face, trying to read it for any sign of deceit. Unfortunately, the thin lips and tiny black eyes gave nothing away.

'Okay, you have me alone. What do you want?'

'I know that the Witch Mother searches for you, Lord Crow. I also know that you wish to be free and have a mortal life. I can help you with these things.'

'And I am guessing you want me to do something in return?'

'Oh but it is such a simple task. Very simple indeed. I will give you the secrets that you so desire and all you have to do in return is destroy the Witch Mother.'

'Destroy her?' Tobias blurted in surprise. 'But I thought you were one of her allies.'

'Things can change, my lord, and I would now benefit greatly if she was to be no more.'

'Why should I trust you?'

'Look at me. I am no threat. I am nothing but a despicable worm who could not compare to the power of the mighty

Tyringar. Indeed, I am merely a pawn in the games of the other Masters. A piece that they move without care.'

'So I kill the Witch Mother and then I can return to a normal life?'

Even as he spoke them, Tobias knew the words sounded truly ridiculous. The very idea of killing the Witch Mother was beyond crazy, yet despite this, Dvesh's face lit up with excitement.

'Yes, yes. That is it.'

'And if I do this, you will have eliminated both Tyringar and the Witch Mother without ever putting yourself at risk?'

'Well, that is the game we play is it not?'

Tobias thought for a moment. Despite the shade of the spire, the heat of the sun felt like it was growing, and the dryness of the air caught in his throat each time he took a breath. He was deeply uncomfortable with both the conversation and the location, but this all seemed to be exactly what he wanted.

What did it matter if Dvesh gained some control? Tobias didn't care what happened in the other realms, he just wanted his life back.

'Okay,' he said. 'What exactly is this deal?'

'Oh, my lord, it is so simple. You see, the Witch Mother already has an agent watching you. A Wraith.'

'What's a Wraith?'

'It is a spirit which must inhabit the physical form of another. This is the danger, my lord. It could be anyone in your world, watching you and waiting for the right moment to strike. The perfect opportunity when it can not only slay the mighty Tyringar but also retrieve Fear Bane and Hexalbion for the Witch Mother's pleasure.'

Dvesh rubbed his hands together excitedly and licked his thin lips with a long slick tongue. He was enjoying this and he was not trying to hide it.

'But this is the Witch Mother's folly,' he continued. 'After your last encounter, she now believes that Tyringar can only be defeated by a weapon of great power, and so she has gifted one to this Wraith. If you can retrieve this weapon and bring it to me, we can use it against her instead.'

Tobias listened and his blood ran cold. The idea that the Witch Mother had found him, and that one of these Wraiths was watching him without him ever knowing was a terrifying one. Despite this, it sounded like there was hope and he needed to know more. He opened his mouth to speak but Dvesh raised a crooked hand to stop him.

'I do not know who this Wraith will be in your world, but if you find and slay it, you will have the key to your desires. You will be free, Lord Crow. We will have a weapon that can defeat the Witch Mother.'

'But won't she just be reborn?' Tobias asked.

'Very astute my lord. You are indeed one of great intelligence. Yes, her soul will be reborn but I can deal with such trivial matters. You just have to find that weapon.'

Dvesh walked forward, picking his way down the rocks and closing the distance between him and Tobias. The Shadow Hunters watched eagerly but didn't move.

Once he was just a few steps away, Dvesh held out one of his gnarled hands.

'Do we have a deal, my lord?'

Tobias froze. He knew he could not trust Dvesh, but the deal felt like an honest one, and it did offer Tobias everything he wanted. He could live his life without ever having the worry of being hunted.

He raised his own hand and was just about to shake on the deal when he realised that everything around him had frozen.

Dvesh stood completely still, unblinking and no breath escaping from between his sneering lips. The Shadow Hunter's atop the rise were also completely motionless. Their bodies stiff, their eyes motionless, and their tails frozen mid swing. Even loose pebbles which had been bouncing down the bank were hanging in place in the air. Only Tobias seemed capable of moving.

Panic gnawing at his stomach, he began searching around frantically for a reason why time appeared to have stopped. It was clearly not Dvesh's doing and the thought that something else might be here caused his heart to quicken and the orange energy around Fear Bane to flash ever brighter.

'I am impressed,' said a voice.

Tobias spun around in its direction and was face to face with a tall, slender woman in a luminous white gown. Her dark skin and black hair didn't just reflect the dim light, but absorbed it and radiated it back out like a brilliant aura of angelic purity.

Chapter 22

'Avesria!' Tobias blurted. She was the last person he had expected to see here.

Avesria smiled. 'You have grown into your power considerably since our last meeting,' she said.

Her voice was still as lilting and melodic as the last time they had met and her appearance was as stunning as ever. An elegant and graceful poise, long hair flowing down to her neck in gentle waves, and soft copper skin glistening as if touched by morning dew.

The visage was enough to take his breath away and he struggled to think of what to say. She had helped him last time, but with her cryptic answers, strange riddles, and half truths, he had never worked out if he could trust her or not. Not to mention the fact she apparently had the power to freeze time.

Unsure what to do, he was about to turn to Hex for advice when he remembered that Hex was gone.

'I am sorry,' Avesria said while Tobias was looking at the empty space on his chest where the stone had been. 'But I wish to speak to you in private, and we do not have much time. I cannot hold this spell for long.'

'Did you know?' Tobias blurted. 'About Hex killing my parents? About who I am?' It was a question that had burned in his mind since he had found out himself.

'I did.'

'Why didn't you tell me?'

'You were not ready to hear it. I had no idea how you would react or whether you could see past the actions of our dear Hexalbion. You still needed him if you were to escape.'

'Is that why you gave me Fear Bane? Because you knew who I was?'

'I knew you were born from Tyringar if that is what you mean. I could sense his presence the moment you entered the Underlands. That does not mean you are him though. He is within you, but you have proven yourself stronger than anyone could ever have expected. You can control who, or what, you want to be.'

More and more questions raced through Tobias' mind. He had so much he wanted to ask her. But one question fought its way to the surface and escaped his mouth first. 'Who are you?'

'A very curious question,' Avesria replied with a slight tilt of her head. 'But we do not have time for such things. You are in danger and I wish to help you.'

'Dvesh has told me about the Wraith and he has offered to help me kill the Witch Mother.'

'Dvesh intends to betray you. He desires to rise in the ranks of the Masters and to do that, he needs both the power of Greed and Fear. Once you kill the Witch Mother for him, he will kill you.'

'So what can I do?'

'You can not accept his deal. You must escape this place with your friends and defeat the Wraith. Beyond this, your path is still shrouded in uncertainty.'

'But what if Dvesh can help me get my life back?'

Avesria leaned in and locked eyes with Tobias. As she did, he felt an intense calm wash over his body and the energy around Fear Bane dispersed in a fine mist.

'Dvesh will not help you,' she said with an air of intensity. 'He desires only suffering and revenge. The other Masters treat him as badly as he treats others and he will not rest until they are punished. In his mind Tyringar was the worst of them, and as far as he is concerned, you are Tyringar.'

'Could you not kill him now?' Tobias asked. The thought of coldly killing anyone while they were helpless didn't feel right, but if Dvesh was as bad as she was saying, maybe it would be for the best.

'I cannot. Even if such a thing was in my power, it is taking all I have just to appear to you in this way, and the longer I stay, the more likely it is that I will be found.'

Tobias turned away from Avesria and looked back at Dvesh. With his oily skin and warped form, he was completely the opposite of her in almost every way. Tobias knew he had to trust one of them and Avesria had helped him escape from the Underlands.

'What about the Wraith?' He asked her.

'A Wraith is a vile creature made by twisting the souls of mortals into tortured remnants of what they once were. Dvesh has a particular knack for the art, but even his creations are not perfect. They must inhabit a physical form.'

'That is what Dvesh told me,' Tobias admitted. 'It could be anyone.'

'Indeed,' Avesria smiled slightly and Tobias got the feeling he had said something silly but he couldn't figure out what it might be.

'So what do I do?'

Tobias could feel a knot forming in his stomach. How could he possibly fight a Wraith, especially if he couldn't even tell who it was.

Avesria stepped even closer and placed a gentle hand on his shoulder. It felt cool, even through his clothes.

'Do not fear,' she whispered into his ear. 'The Wraith may have been their biggest mistake.'

Pulling back she reached into her sleeve and pulled out a long rolled piece of parchment.

'I have sacrificed much to find this,' she said, handing it out to Tobias. 'It is the Scroll of Gluasad. Read it while pressing Hexalbion's stone to the host of the Wraith and you will not only force the creature out but also establish him in its place.'

'It will free him?'

Avesria smiled again. 'It will free him.'

Tobias held the scroll tight in his hand. This was something that he had been hoping to find ever since he had made his promise to Hex, and now he had it. All he had to do was use it. All he had to do was find the Wraith. The knot returned to his stomach.

'Now, you must go,' Avesria said while glancing up into the Shadow Hunters. Their tails were beginning to twitch and their eyes locking onto Tobias. 'My grip is loosening.'

Before Tobias could respond, Avesria had taken him by the shoulders and was guiding him swiftly back in the direction of the Gate. She was gliding along behind him as if her feet did not even touch the floor and her grip on his shoulders was firm yet soft.

'Your friends are already back and waiting for you. They are keeping the Gate open for you, but it is still a long way to reach it. I can only hold Dvesh for a moment longer.'

She kissed him on the forehead and then pushed hard, sending him stumbling into a run.

'Go now Tobias,' she called after him. 'Never give in.'

Chapter 23

The loose dirt and sand of Vikessa shifted under Tobias' feet as he ran. It was slowing him down but his boots dug in hard and kept him moving. No matter how much he was panicking, each time that he thought he might slip, his feet always seemed to find sure footing. He had no idea how long Avesria would hold Dvesh and his Shadow Hunters back, but he knew he couldn't afford to lose any time.

'Don't look back,' Tobias began chanting to himself as he spotted one of the stone markers he and his friends had left to signpost their way.

'Don't think of the danger.'

'Keep your head low.'

'Keep running.'

It felt like a lifetime since he had used that mantra, but it came back to him as naturally as breathing. Just reciting it soothed him and gave him something to focus on other than the worry of what may be catching up behind him.

Another stone marker came into view in the distance. A short tower of stones with the widest of them at the top. He recognised it instantly because he remembered thinking it was a bad idea when Kayt made it so top heavy. Now he was glad to see it. Knowing that the edge of the spire's shadow laid just a short distance beyond, he headed straight at the pile of stones and rushed past.

Continuing to push himself on while ignoring the weakness of his legs, Tobias emerged back into the harsh light of the sun as the shadow abruptly ended. It was like hitting a wall of heat and he had forgotten just how overpowering it was. The sweat that had been forming all over his body from the exertion of the run instantly evaporated, creating an icy sensation on his skin which lasted only a moment before it prickled and burned.

Running in the shade of the spire had been tiring, but now it was like the air itself was resisting him. To make matters worse, the sound of low growls was also beginning to reach his ears.

Despite his mantra and all his better judgement, Tobias instinctively glanced back over his shoulder. The pack of Shadow Hunters was bounding across the sand with incredible speed and the gap was closing fast.

It didn't matter how much energy Tobias could manifest, there was no way he would be fast enough to fight five agile predators when he was already suffering such fatigue. He needed a single powerful attack. It was going to take everything he had and he would only have one chance. Any more and he doubted he would even have the strength to keep moving.

His knuckles whitened around the handle of Fear Bane as he reached deep into the back of his mind and pulled forth all the memories of horror from his life. His uncle, the demons of the Underlands, the Witch Mother, and finally, his parents death. The last image in particular conjured a deep emotional response. He siphoned every shred of it into the weapon, but holding on to so much power while still trying to keep up his pace in the unforgiving heat felt like more than his body could take.

Gritting his teeth and forcing his brain to ignore the agony of his protesting limbs, he swung Fear Bane through the air behind him and screamed in fury as he released every shred of the power he had mustered. It produced a glowing wave of energy which engulfed the area in a fountain of sand and stone. As the yellow grains settled back to the floor, he could see four of the cat creatures laying in crooked black heaps, blood pooling around them.

Without stopping, Tobias scanned the area for any sign of his fifth pursuer, but there was nothing there. No body in the sand, no injured beast still giving chase, not even any blood to mark that it might have been hurt. To make matters worse, after the exertion of his attack, exhaustion was swiftly beginning to rob Tobias of any speed he had left. He knew he had to make it to the Gate before the missing Shadow Hunter caught up to him, but he wasn't sure if his body had the reserves to carry him there.

Tripping slightly and with the muscles of his legs threatening to give way with every step, he pushed himself on. The pain was excruciating and his mind kept drifting into foggy confusion because of the fatigue, but he could not give in. Fear was once again his strength. He knew that if he stopped, if he gave in to the overwhelming desire to just lay down and surrender, Dvesh would have him. The fear of what would come next was all the motivation he needed. His mind summoned up thoughts of being trapped in this realm, suffering eternal torture, and never seeing his friends again. These thoughts fueled his fear and in turn his fear fueled him.

With a grunt Tobias stumbled on until the chamber which housed the Gate came into view. The shattered walls and scattered rubble still covered the ground around it. What remained of the structure was also beginning to crumble, but in that moment, the building felt like a beacon of hope.

Tobias' left leg lost its balance and he collapsed to the ground. A part of him wanted to stay there, knees and hands pressed into the sand and his head hung low.

The ground was hot against his skin and the air felt like it was thick enough to choke him. Ragged panting desperately tried to draw it into his lungs, causing a tight burning sensation in his chest. Despite this, the respite of being motionless, if even for a moment, felt good. But Tobias knew he couldn't stay on the ground. He had to get up. He had to keep running.

Lifting himself awkwardly back to his feet, Tobias stumbled a couple of times before he finally managed to lock his legs into place and straighten his back. The effort caused his eyes to water, and as this moisture was consumed by the heat, it was replaced by a dry stinging sensation. He rubbed his eyes with the back of his hand before looking back to the chamber, and the Shadow Hunter which was now standing guard in front of it.

There was no way past the sleek black creature. Certainly not in the state Tobias had now found himself. He had no strength in his muscles to move quickly, and the only energy he could conjure around Fear Bane was a meager strand of vapour, almost too faint to see.

The beast must have sensed this weakness because it visibly relaxed its stance and began prowling forward without the slightest hint of trepidation. Circling Tobias, it watched him as a tom cat might eye an injured bird. Then it leapt forward and Tobias was forced to dive backwards.

It was more of a fall than a dodge but Tobias did manage to narrowly avoid the glistening black claws as they swept past his face. Landing heavily onto his back, Tobias watched as the Shadow Hunter deftly came to land before leaping through the air once again. He could do nothing but raise Fear Bane, close his eyes and pray that it would at the very least be a fast and painless end.

'Pathetic!' the voice in the back of his mind hissed at him. There was so much venom and anger in the word that Tobias physically winced as it spoke.

'We are better than this,' the voice continued. 'We can not be killed so easily. We must not!'

Tobias could sense the presence creeping into his consciousness, trying to take control. He desperately tried to fight it back. He knew he was about to die, but the idea of giving in to this thing was far more terrifying than death. He could feel its hatred and fury and he knew it wanted to bring destruction with it. Unfortunately, Tobias did not have the strength or energy to hold it at bay and the only way he knew to prevent it from taking hold was to save his own life.

'Get out of my head!' Tobias screamed.

His eyes snapped open just in time to see a look of confusion break across the Shadow Hunter's face as it bore down on him. Then an explosion of orange and crimson erupted from the creature's back and it fell limp to the floor.

Chapter 24

Tobias was unsure how long he had been robbed of his senses, but he knew that after killing the Shadow Hunter, his exhaustion had finally taken its toll and he had lost consciousness.

Regardless of whether his blackout had been hours or mere moments, regaining focus on his surroundings was not easy. Darkness kept creeping into his vision and as he stood, dizziness threatened to send him straight back down. His head spun and the ground felt like it was tilting beneath his feet.

Fear Bane rested in the sand a few feet away and when Tobias bent down to retrieve the weapon, he had to brace himself to prevent another fall.

'You have impressed me yet again, Lord Crow.'

Dvesh's raspy voice carried on the still air and Tobias had to search out which direction it was coming from. Atop a low rise, not far away, stood the gnarled Master of Vikessa.

'Why won't you just let me leave?' Tobias asked, forcing the words out of his dry throat.

'Leave?' Dvesh asked in mock surprise. 'Why would you want to leave when we are having so much fun?'

'So what now? You are going to kill me?'

'Maybe,' Dvesh replied. Then scratching his chin in thought, he added, 'but maybe I will fetch your companions back from the mortal realm first. I could have you watch as I strip the flesh from their bones. Now that might be entertaining.'

Anger churned in Tobias stomach and he tried to take a step forward, towards Dvesh. As he did, dizziness took him once again and he had to stop before he fell.

'You will leave them alone,' he demanded instead.

Dvesh's thin lips twisted into a wicked grin which bared rows of sharp pointed teeth. 'I don't think you are in much of a position to argue.'

'I will kill you,' Tobias said. He hoped he sounded as threatening as he intended. 'I have already killed your Shadow Hunters,'

'This is true,' Dvesh replied. 'But such poor, simple creatures could never hope to defeat the great Tyringar. Even if you are but a mere shade of your former self. Those feeble things were little more than a distraction for you. Pawns intended only to keep you here. The honour of killing you will be mine and mine alone.' Dvesh looked up and locked eyes with Tobias. 'I say 'alone', but I am no fool. I will, of course, have help.'

As if those very words were their command, a dozen more shapes began appearing on the rise alongside Dvesh. Each one was a grotesque goblin shaped Porigast, but unlike the one Tobias had met before, these were larger, covered in dark iron armour, and were carrying a long serrated sword in each hand. They clambered up the low hill and grinned down at Tobias.

'Any last words, Tyringar?' Dvesh asked.

'I am not Tyringar,' Tobias replied through gritted teeth.

There was no command word and no signal. The Porigasts just seemed to know it was time. With a cacophony of shrill screams, they launched themselves forward, and Tobias found himself facing down a wall of gnashing teeth and wicked blades. The sudden realisation that he lacked both the energy and strength to win caused his legs to buckle slightly and his skin to become slick with cold sweat.

'Release me!' Demanded the dark voice in the back of his mind.

'No.'

'Release me or you will die.'

'I will not give in to you. I won't.'

'RELEASE ME!' The voice reverberated in his mind. It was so loud that it caused his entire body to throb with pain.

Looking up at the swarm of death which was nearly on top of him, then down at the distant whisper of fear which he could draw into Fear Bane, Tobias could see no other option. He would have to give in. He would have to release the full power of the thing that lurked in the depths of his soul. He had no choice.

He felt the savage, primal rage rising. He sensed the power creeping through his muscles. He was just about to let go and release it all. Then something happened. Another shape joined the fight.

It was fast and deadly and it darted between the Porigasts like a chaotic whirlwind of carnage. All Tobias could make out from this newcomer was a swirling mass of grey and white. Still, one by one, the Porigasts fell to its fury.

The corpse of one porigast was flung through the air in Tobias' direction and landed at his feet. He looked down at the bloody form and saw that its face was covered in dozens of tiny cuts which bled out onto the dry soil.

Another Porigast fell, then another, and another. Until the only ones which remained began to squeal in fright and flee.

'Fight you wretches,' Dvesh screamed at them, but none were listening.

'Fine,' the gnarled little creature hissed. 'I'll finish this myself.'

He moved forward towards Tobias and raised a clawed hand. A purple tar-like substance began secreting from his fingers and trailed out into the air like snakes. His face was even more contorted than before and he lurched across the ground with an awkward limping gait.

One of the purple tendrils lashed out towards Tobias, but before it could hit, the newcomer stepped in the way and batted it aside. Dvesh hissed in fury.

Tobias, now looking up at the back of his saviour, recognised the dark grey robe of the creature from his dreams. His blood felt like it had frozen in his veins as the featureless, alabaster face turned to him and in its unmistakable slow drawl, it said 'I am here for you Tobias Crow.'

Dvesh launched another tendril, and this time it was the faceless man who hissed as the thick tacky tentacle lashed across his shoulder and caused a spurt of crimson blood to fill the air.

'Get out of my way,' Dvesh commanded.

'You can not have him,' the stranger replied.

Then the two rushed each other.

Tobias watched in horror as the two creatures of nightmare battled. He had no idea what would happen when either one won, but neither appeared to be getting the upper hand. Dvesh was not graceful but his snake-like tendrils were fast and they stabbed and slashed with terrifying accuracy. Each time one struck, it drew a thick streak of blood.

On the other side, the faceless stranger was both quick and nimble. He darted around, rushing in close to place an open palm against Dvesh's body before dodging backwards to avoid an attack. Each time his palm made contact, the grizzly mouths in his hands would rip another chunk from Dvesh's flesh.

Desperation growing, Dvesh began launching more and more attacks but each one looked like it tired him a little more. He was running out of energy and he knew it. It was only a matter of time before he wouldn't be able to keep up with the onslaught.

'I am a Master,' Dvesh rasped.

'You are nothing,' the faceless man's voice replied in a calm, measured tone. 'A traitor. A slave to those stronger than you.'

'Well if I must die, I am taking him with me.'

Dvesh jumped awkwardly around the faceless man, and though he landed heavily on the ground, his life energy seeping out, he still managed to send one last tendril stabbing out towards Tobias.

'No!' the faceless man yelled, and it almost looked like he tried to get in the way of the attack, but he was too slow. The point of the tendril drove into Tobias chest, just below his ribs, and burst out from his back before fading into nothing.

Tobias barely had time to acknowledge the burning pain of the injury before he fell unconscious. The last thing he saw was the porcelain skin of the faceless man looking down at him, and the frothing maws in swollen palms reaching towards his face.

Chapter 25

Tobias awoke in a small room. It was a gloomy, empty space, which while illuminated in a dull glow, had no visible light source. No furniture or decoration broke the monotony of the smooth walls and it felt like being in a featureless box with no way out.

Standing in the corner, watching him with an eyeless gaze, was the faceless stranger.

Instinctively Tobias reached down to his chest and felt for the wound Dvesh had inflicted. It was not there. No torn flesh. No blood. Not even a scar. There was nothing on his back either.

'We are in a dream,' the faceless man said. 'That is why we have no injuries. But make no mistake, in the real world, you are fighting for your life.'

'Who are you?' Tobias asked.

'I am Streth'na'fell. Last of the Nightmare Court, and eternal servant of the Nightmare Lord.'

'Nightmare Lord?'

'You, Tobias. You are the rightful Nightmare Lord, and my master.'

'So you don't want to hurt me?'

'No. I exist only to serve and protect you. I have already returned you to the mortal realm. The girl is trying to help you.'

'You mean Kayt?'

'I do not know her name, but her dreams smell of rose and sage.'

Though the comment was odd and more than a little creepy, Tobias put it to the back of his mind. 'What about Dvesh?' He asked. 'What happened to him?'

'He escaped. He will not last long though. Not once the Witch Mother learns of his failure.'

'So what now? Am I dying?'

'Only if that is your desire. You are the Lord of Nightmares. You have the power to heal yourself.'

'How.'

'Just will it and it will be so. You are the master of your own body Tobias. Tell it what to do.'

Tobias closed his eyes and imagined his body healing. He desperately tried to picture the holes in his chest and back closing up and the bleeding stopping.

'I don't think it is working,' he said when he felt no difference.

'That is because you still think of your power's as purely destructive. You have the power of nightmares. You can manifest them as a creative energy just as easily as a deadly weapon.'

Streth'na'fell leaned in closer, and Tobias fought back the urge to flinch away. Despite believing that this creature meant him no harm, he still felt uncomfortable at the things proximity.

'Close your eyes,' Streth'na'fell instructed.

Tobias did as he was told.

'Now reach out and feel the fear around you.'

Again, Tobias followed the instructions. At first there was nothing, but as he concentrated, the sensation of fear began to creep into his mind. It was not his own fear though. It was the fear of those around him. Kayt, Jay, Scavenger, and even Hex. Each of them was terrified for their friend who was bleeding out in front of them.

'I can feel it,' he admitted.

'Good. Now take that fear and absorb it. Pull it into your body and make it real. Make it heal you.'

Tobias mentally tugged at the energy around him. It was like threads, twirling through the air without purpose. He took each in turn and made them solid, much as he did when creating shards in battle. Once solid, he imagined pulling the strands in. Weaving them through his wound and pulling it closed. He felt the air around him quiver and opening his eyes, Tobias saw a shimmer fill the room and distort everything in it. Including Streth'na'fell.

'What is happening?' he asked as the shimmer spread.

'Your body is healing,' Streth'na'fell replied. 'Soon you will return to it.'

'But I have so many more questions.'

'I will answer them in time, but for now I must remain in Vikessa and destroy the Gate. I will find you again.'

'Wait,' Tobias called out, but it was already too late. Both the room and Streth'na'fell were fading and Tobias was waking up.

Chapter 26

'Tobias,' Kayt cried out when his eyes opened. 'Where am I?'

'You are home. Jay carried you.' Tears welled up in Kayt's eyes, and as she spoke through heavy sobs, she kept wiping them away with the backs of her hands.

'You were bleeding so much. I wanted to take you to the hospital, or ring an ambulance, or something. But Hex said we couldn't. He said that we had to get you here, so that's what we did. Are you okay? Please say you are. We should have taken you to a hospital. I know…'

Tobias lifted an arm and clutched her shoulder. 'I'm fine.'

'But how? I don't understand.'

'Neither do I,' Tobias confessed.

Pulling himself up into a sitting position, he expected to feel some form of pain or discomfort where Dvesh had struck him, but there was none. Looking at his bare chest and stomach, there wasn't even a scar.

'Am I naked?' He asked, suddenly realising that the only thing covering him up was a blood stained blanket.

Kayt's face turned bright red and she looked away while pushing her glasses further up her nose. 'Your uncle undressed you. He was looking for the injury but he said it was already healing. I didn't see anything. I promise. It was just him and Scavenger. I waited outside with Jay and Hex.'

'It's okay,' Tobias laughed. 'But it would be nice if I could put some clothes on.'

'Oh yeah. Sure. I mean, sorry. I'll just wait outside.'

Her skin turning ever more crimson by the second, Kayt jumped up and rushed for the bedroom door. She turned back just long enough to say, 'We are all really glad you're okay,' before stepping through and out of sight.

Tobias smiled as he watched his friend leave. Not only was he alive, but it sounded like everyone he cared about was also okay. He had survived again.

Then his smile faded as he remembered everything else that had happened. Nearly giving into the voice at the back of his mind, the faceless Streth'na'fell, and Avesria's warning about the Wraith. The idea that someone in his life was a monster working for the Witch Mother caused an involuntary shudder to rush up his spine.

Climbing out of his bed, he moved over to the wardrobe and pulled out some clothes. His mind was far too preoccupied by his thoughts to care which clothes he picked so he just grabbed the closest ones. A plain red t-shirt and joggers.

Pulling on the t-shirt, he replayed the events in Vikessa over and over in his head. He was unsure if Dvesh really was dead, or if Streth'na'fell had destroyed the gate, but his primary concern had to be on finding and stopping the Wraith.

'The scroll,' he blurted as he suddenly realised he had no idea where it was. Frantically, he searched his room before darting out into the living room.

Both Jay and Kayt were sitting on the sofa with Scavenger in Kayt's lap. Hex's stone rested atop the television alongside the silver circlet, and Tobias' uncle was pacing backwards and forwards between the front door and the kitchen. All of them looked up as Tobias exploded into the room and began searching behind every piece of furniture.

'What's wrong, Toby?' His uncle asked. The effort of being up and on his feet for so long had drained the colour from his skin and replaced it with a thin sheen of sweat.

'Where is my bag?' Tobias asked as he rummaged through the coats hanging beside the front door.

'It's here,' Jay replied, holding the bag up in one hand. 'It came through the Gate with you. Are you okay?'

Tobias didn't reply but snatched the bag out of Jay's hand and ripped it open. Scavenger's blanket sat at the top and beneath that was the empty water bottles and various packets or wrappers from his snacks. He pulled each out and discarded them on the floor until he reached the bundled cloth wrapped around Fear Bane.

The sight of the weapon was a relief and instantly eased tension Tobias hadn't realised he was feeling until it was gone, but he still needed the scroll.

Eventually, becoming far too impatient, Tobias pulled Fear Bane out and placed it on the coffee table before upending the bag and dumping the rest of its contents on the floor. The last thing to emerge was a rolled piece of yellow parchment.

'What is that?' Hex asked as Tobias picked it up.

'Avesria gave it to me. She said there is something called a Wraith possessing someone close to me and this can stop it.'

Tobias turned and looked at Hex before adding, 'She said it could place you in the body instead.'

'It can free me?' Even without facial expressions, the shock was clear in Hex's voice.

'I think so.'

'What's a Wraith,' his uncle asked. His brow was furrowed and his lips parted in both worry and confusion.

Kayt stood up and placed Scavenger on the floor before taking Tobias' uncle by the elbow and guiding him to the sofa. 'Come and sit down Mr. Crow,' she told him, and he did as he was instructed without any resistance.

Once his uncle had relaxed slightly in his seat, Tobias stood in front of them all and began recounting what had happened. He told them about Dvesh, Avesria, the Wraith, and how Avesria had helped him escape. He didn't mention Streth'na'fell just yet however. He wasn't sure how they would take it, and wasn't entirely sure how to handle it himself yet. Instead he told them that he had stumbled through the Gate himself after Dvesh had wounded him.

All of them listened intently as Tobias spoke and even his uncle looked up at him with sadness in his eyes.

'I wish I was better able to protect you,' he said.

'This is bad news indeed,' Hex interrupted as if Tobias' uncle hadn't even spoken. 'A Wraith really could be anyone.'

'Could it be one of us?' Kayt asked.

'I hadn't really thought about that,' Tobias replied, suddenly very aware that he had told the people in this room almost everything about himself and allowed them to get closer to him than anyone else.

'It's not one of us,' Jay said matter of factly, and Kayt looked at him with a puzzled expression.

'How do you know?' She asked.

'Well it's not Tobias, otherwise that would defeat the point. Hex and Scavenger are obviously not an issue. And as for us two or Mr. Crow, we have had plenty of chances to kill the wimp and take his stuff, but we haven't. So obviously it isn't us.'

'That actually makes sense.'

'I'm not as dumb as people think I am.'

Tobias listened to the two speaking. He didn't know whether Jay actually made sense or whether he just wanted it to be true. In the end he decided that the other boy was right. If the Wraith was in Kayt, Jay or his uncle, they could have easily killed him and taken Fear Bane and Hex by now. That still left one question though.

'So who is it?'

Jay shrugged.

'What about Mr Leach?' Kayt asked.

'Nah,' Jay replied. 'He is too obvious.'

'That's what I mean. He is horrible, he likes tormenting kids and it was him who found us in the haunted hallway.'

'Yeah but I have watched enough movies to know that when you have a secret villain, it is never the clearly evil one. It's always the sweet, innocent one who is pretending to be nice so that he can get close.'

'Okay,' Kayt replied thoughtfully. Then turning to Tobias, she asked, 'Who has been really nice to you?'

'I don't really know. Everyone has just kind of ignored me apart from you two.'

'What about that Head Teacher of yours?' Hex asked, breaking his silence.

'You mean Mr Fenwick?'

'He seemed a little too friendly to me.'

'Oh yeah, he is definitely the secret villain type,' Jay added.

'I don't know. I only really spoke to him on my first day. I haven't had much to do with him since then.'

'Yeah but he is always there isn't he,' said Jay with a smug smile as if he had just solved the world's most complicated case.

'He's the Head Teacher,' Kayt replied. 'He has to be there. It's his school.'

'I know but you have to admit, he is weirdly cheerful. No one can be that happy all the time. Besides, who else could it be?'

'Just because he is happy…' Kayt began but Tobias had stopped listening to the conversation.

The thought of anyone around him being a servant of the Witch Mother caused every hair on his body to prickle. And the idea that they were just watching him live his life while plotting his death, made him feel sick to his stomach.

His mind raced to think of everyone who was close to him but it wasn't a long list. If it had been his uncle, Kayt or Jay, he would be dead already, but who else could it be?

He had to admit, the only other one who made sense was Mr. Fenwick.

'...So just because he lives alone, he has to be evil?' Kayt asked.

'You have to admit, it would make being evil easier,' Jay replied.

'I'm not sure that even makes sense.'

'Look, all I am saying is maybe we should check him out.'

'What about Mary?' Hex offered.

'Who is Mary?' Jay asked.

Tobias' uncle shook his head. 'She is a friend who lives down the hall,' he replied weakly. 'She does the shopping for us and spends time with me when Tobias is out. She has helped us through a really hard time.'

Jay scratched his chin in thought. 'Well she is definitely another possibility.'

'She is a friend,' Tobias' uncle protested.

'The Wraith would want you to think that.'

Tobias' uncle shifted in his seat and began nervously rubbing his hands together. 'This is crazy,' he said as his sweating intensified. Tobias had seen this before. It was all getting too much for the man and he was getting anxious. He would be demanding a drink next.

Before he could step forward to try and calm his Uncle, Tobias was interrupted by Kayt who moved across in front of him and put a hand on his uncle's shoulder.

'It's okay, Mr. Crow.' She said in a soft and calming tone. 'I know it is all very scary but Tobias knows what he is doing and he has all of us to help him. Would you like a glass of water?'

Tobias' uncle nodded and Kayt rushed off to fetch a drink from the kitchen. After taking a sip, he looked back up at Tobias and said, 'sorry.'

'It's okay,' Tobias replied.

'When you have all quite finished,' Hex said after Kayt had perched herself on the arm of the sofa next to Tobias' uncle. 'We should have a good look at that scroll.'

'Good idea,' Jay said with a nod. Then grabbing the parchment out of Tobias' hand, he immediately began to unroll it. 'This scroll is nonsense. Look, it's all just scrawls and scribbles.'

'You need special glasses to read it,' Tobias told him. 'I have some.'

Tobias began rummaging through everything he had tipped out onto the floor, but before he had a chance to hand over the Revelare Lenses, Kayt grabbed the paper and began turning it over in her hands. Then she began reading out loud.

'The Scroll of Gluasad. Ritual of the Snared Soul.'

'Wait a minute, you can read that scrawl? Jay asked in obvious shock.

'That shouldn't be possible,' Hex added.

Tobias didn't say anything. He just stood there, holding out the Revelare Lenses and letting his mouth hang open.

'What?' Kayt asked, looking between each of them. 'It all looks very clear to me. It says we need to hold the soul stone in one hand while touching the flesh of the host with the other. Then we just need to read the words here.' She pointed to a section of the scroll which looked like a series of idle doodles to everyone else.

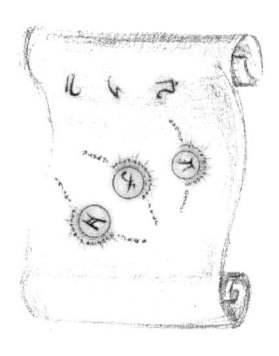

'You can really read that?' Tobias asked.

'Yes. Why is it so surprising?'

'Because nobody else here can,' Hex replied impatiently. 'Texts like these are written in truly ancient languages which take a lifetime to learn. That is why archivists like myself use the lenses.'

'I don't know.' Kayt gave a dismissive shrug of her shoulders. 'I guess I'm just a natural.'

A deep sigh emanated from Hex's stone. 'There is clearly more to it than that, but we do not have the time or resources to examine this any further. We will have to address it after the current threat is dealt with.'

Under his breath, Hex added to Tobias, 'Keep an eye on her.' But Tobias ignored him.

'What else does it say?' He asked Kayt.

Kayt began pointing to different sections of the scroll, some of which looked like little more than crude pictures to everyone else. 'This bit here is what I just said. These are the words we have to read. And this here says that if the host already contains its true soul, both it and the one from the soul stone will occupy the body.'

'What if the host doesn't have its true soul?' Hex asked.

'Like the Wraith?'

'Exactly.'

Kayt spent a few seconds reading over the paper. Her finger traced along lines as she read and she stopped once to adjust her glasses. Eventually, she looked up.

'If the host already contains a soul which is not native to the body, it will replace the one released from the soul stone and become forever trapped in a prison intended for another.'

'So this really could release me?' Hex asked.

'Looks like it,' Kayt replied as she rolled up the scroll and passed it back to Tobias. 'I know we still have loads to figure out, but I should probably be getting home. It's late and my dad will be wondering where I am.'

'Yeah, my Gran will probably have tea ready too,' Jay added.

Tobias looked out the window at the darkening sky. He hadn't realised how late it was, and after everything they had been through, of course his friends wanted to get back and see their families.

'Thank you for everything,' Tobias told them both as he walked them to the front door.

'No problem,' Kayt replied. 'And don't worry. We will find the Wraith.'

'Yeah, we will find it and smash it.' Jay added, punching his fist into the palm of his hand to add emphasis to the last words.

Kayt rolled her eyes and pushed Jay through the door. 'Erm, yeah. Something like that.'

'Hey,' Jay protested but he didn't resist.

Just before Kayt disappeared into the corridor outside she leaned back into the apartment and shouted, 'Bye Mr. Crow.' Then to Tobias, she added 'See you at school.'

'Yeah, see you later wimp,' Jay added with a friendly punch to Tobias' shoulder.

Tobias grinned and punched Jay back. It was still like hitting a bag of bricks but at least the other boy grunted from the impact. Jay gave Tobias one last smile before running to catch up to Kayt.

'Hey, wait up,' he called to her. Then the two of them disappeared around a corner and out of sight.

Tobias looked down at Scavenger standing by his side.

'You hungry?' he asked.

Scavenger squealed happily and ran in to find his food bowl.

Chapter 27

After Kayt and Jay had left, Tobias helped his uncle to bed and cooked them both pie and chips for tea. His uncle hadn't spoken much after the others had gone but both his pain and worry were clear on his face. Tobias decided to eat his tea in his uncle's room so that he could be with him.

Leaving Scavenger to enjoy a large bowl of pie crust and gravy, Tobias carried his tray into his uncle's room and sat in the chair beside the bed. His uncle was propped up with a pillow at his back and his own tray on his lap. Neither of them ate much and they prodded at more of the food than they actually placed into their mouths.

'I didn't take any of this as seriously as I should have,' Tobias' uncle said. 'I should have listened more when you came home last time.'

'You were ill.'

'I was a drunk.' his uncle said flatly. 'A drunk, an idiot and a vile man. I know I am lucky that you came back at all.'

'A part of me didn't want to,' Tobias confessed.

'I can never express how glad I am that you did.'

'We are family,' Tobias said. As the words were spoken, a deep sadness filled his uncle's eyes.

'You are the only family I have left, Toby. That is why I can never forgive myself for the way I treated you. Your mother would have been so disappointed in me.'

'You don't talk about them much,' Tobias said. He was hoping to encourage his uncle to say more, but the man just shook his head and stared down at the food on his lap.

'Your dad was a good brother to me,' he said at last. 'And I loved your mother deeply. Losing them was the hardest thing I have ever faced.'

'It was the Witch Mother,' Tobias blurted.

His uncle looked up at him in shock. 'What?'

'She was trying to kill me, but she got them instead.'

'I don't understand, Toby. Why would she want to kill you? She didn't even know you back then did she?'

Tobias went quiet. He wasn't sure what had made him tell his uncle the truth, but now he wasn't sure how much to say.

Picking his words carefully, he looked up at his uncle and met his gaze. 'She thinks I am the reincarnation of one of her enemies. So she sent someone to kill me. She thought I was dead until she met me in the Underlands.'

Tobias saw his uncle's expression darken and his knuckles turned white as he clutched his tray. For a brief, terrifying moment, it reminded Tobias of all the times when his uncle was on the verge of losing his temper and flying into a drunken rage. Instinctively he looked to the door and prepared to run.

Before he could move, however, his uncle reached out and clutched him by the wrist. It was a firm grip but it was not tight or aggressive, and his uncle's face was soft once again.

'It's okay, Toby. I am not mad at you. I would like to see this Witch Mother pay for what she has done to us though.'

'So would I,' Tobias replied.

Releasing Tobias' wrist, his uncle picked up his tray and placed it on the bedside table. 'Is there anything else that I should know?' He asked.

'Nothing important,' Tobias replied.

'Then we should probably talk about this in the morning.'

His uncle slid down to lay flat in the bed and groaned loudly as he eased himself into position.

'Now though, I really need to sleep,' his uncle continued. 'And so do you.'

Tobias nodded. 'Okay uncle.'

He was just about to leave the room when his uncle called out again. 'Tobias.'

'Yeah.'

'I am really sorry. For everything.'

Tobias was unsure what else to say, so he just nodded and went straight to his room. Scavenger was already curled up in his blanket, and Tobias hung hex back on the door. Then he went about his routines.

He checked the window, looked beneath his bed and in his wardrobe, blocked the wardrobe door with his stool and wound his torch. Finally, he kissed the picture of his parents and climbed into bed.

He suddenly felt exhausted. It didn't take long for sleep to take him, and with sleep came the nightmares.

Tobias was walking down a long, narrow corridor. Long fluorescent bulbs provided a dim glow which barely reached the floor and either side of him the walls were dotted with small windows. He looked through the first few that he passed. Inside were people. They were standing completely still, their arms limp by their sides and their eyes closed.

At first Tobias thought that he didn't recognise any of them, but then he noticed teachers from the school, children from his class, and staff in the local shops. These were all people who he had met, but some of them he had only met once or twice and he didn't even know their names.

He continued further down the passage, peering through each window that he passed. A few more he barely knew. The postman, the school receptionist, and Mary from down the hall. Then there was Mr. Buckle, Mr. Leach, Mr. Fenwick, and even Avesria.

The further he went, the closer the people were to his life. He knew what was coming next. His uncle, Kayt, Jay, and Hexalbion. This was Hexalbion from one of Tobias' previous dreams though. When he had been a man and not a soul in a stone. Tobias recognised his sharp angular features and pointed beard beneath long black hair.

Only three more windows remained before the corridor stretched off into complete darkness. He stepped carefully up to the first and looked inside. Two people stood in the gloom. A man and a woman. His parents. Like all the others, they were limp and unconscious but they were holding hands like they were in their photograph.

Tobias wiped a tear from his eye and turned to the next window. Scavenger was sitting on the floor, slumped over so that his chin rested on his round belly and his ears hung loose across his face.

Only one more window to go. But who could be closer to him than Scavenger or his parents? He stepped forward, not quite in front of the glass but close enough that he could lean around and glance inside. Stood with shoulders slumped and head down, was another Tobias.

It was like looking in the mirror. Yet something felt oddly wrong. Everything about this other Tobias looked familiar, but he somehow knew that it wasn't really him.

Taking a step closer and pressing his face to the glass, Tobias tried to make out some small difference that might separate him from this strange figure. Then its eyes opened.

They were not the warm green eyes which Tobias was used to seeing in the mirror. Instead they shone with a burning orange colour with long tendrils of orange smoke drifting lazily out from the corners and coiling around the other Tobias' face.

Tobias took a startled step back, and as he did, the other Tobias took a step forward. A smile crept across its lips.

'What are you?' Tobias asked. His voice quivered and he stumbled back another step, which was once again matched by the thing in front of him. It was almost up to the glass now.

'Whatever do you mean?' It replied. 'I am you.' It sounded like him but its tone was menacing and its smile, sinister.

'You're not me. You can't be.'

'Oh but I can, and I am. I am the real you. The you who fights back. The you who survives.'

'No!' Tobias screamed. 'You are not me!'

The other Tobias began laughing. It started as a low chuckle but as Tobias backed away, it quickly grew until it was a full, manic howling which echoed in every direction.

Tobias turned to run but he was stopped when something grabbed him by the shoulders. It was the faceless form of Streth'na'fell. His long fingers clutched on tight and the gnashing maws on his palms bit deep into Tobias' flesh.

As Streth'na'fell's featureless face leaned in close, his slow voice whispered into Tobias ear. 'Do not worry, Tobias. We will end all of this together.'

Tobias jerked awake, his covers slick with sweat and his hair pasted across his face. It was still dark outside and Scavenger was snoring loudly.

With most of the night still to go, Tobias flicked on his torch, pulled his duvet up over his head, and settled back down for what remained of a very broken and restless sleep.

Chapter 28

'You had a rough night,' Hex said as Tobias climbed out of bed.

'Just some nightmares,' Tobias replied as dismissively as he could manage.

'Do you want to talk about them? I might be able to help.'

Tobias looked over at the stone, hanging from his bedroom door handle. There was so much he hadn't told anyone and he still didn't feel comfortable confiding in Hex anymore than he had to. Despite this, there were so many questions that he needed answers to and denying or hiding what was happening to him wouldn't help.

'Do you know a creature called Streth'na'fell?' Tobias asked at last.

'Yes, but that is not a name I have heard in a very long time. It is not one I am eager to hear again. Why? Did you dream of him?'

'Something like that,' Tobias replied.

'Well, he was not a creature to be taken lightly. According to the accounts I have read, he was created by Tyringar and tasked with leading as his master's right hand. Streth'na'fell was a zealous follower who ultimately died for Tyringar when the Witch Mother purged the Nightmare Court.'

'So he was evil?'

'That is hard to say with a creature like Streth'na'fell. He certainly wasn't good and he was responsible for a great many evil actions, but I wouldn't say that he himself was evil.'

'But how could he do evil things if he wasn't evil?'

'You must understand, he was created to serve. He was driven solely by his loyalty and need to please his master. He did nothing out of cruelty alone, but would think nothing of inflicting cruelty if he thought it would further Tyringar's goals.'

'Were there others in the Nightmare Court?'

'There were dozens. All manner of creatures loyal to the Lord of Nightmares. But the Witch Mother and her allies destroyed them all. Some were even on the Pillar of Souls with me.'

'But Streth'na'fell wasn't?'

'No. My guess is that either she was keeping him somewhere else, she failed to trap his soul, or he didn't have a true soul to begin with because he was a creation of Tyringar.'

Tobias pulled his t-shirt over his head before looping Hex around his neck.

'If you are having dreams about Streth'na'fell, it is not a good sign,' Hex continued. 'Did anything else happen in this nightmare?'

'No, nothing,' Tobias lied.

'You must be careful. You are not Tyringar, but I have no idea how the fragment of his soul could be affecting you. Especially with everything that is happening. We need to stay focused on the task at hand.'

'Don't worry. I will still free you.'

'That is not what I mean.' Hex sounded genuinely offended. 'I do care about you Tobias and I want you to be safe.'

'Yeah, so do I,' Tobias replied before pushing Hex beneath his t-shirt.

Spending the rest of the morning preparing himself for school, Tobias ate breakfast in silence before feeding both Scavenger and his uncle, and heading out the door.

'Morning Tobias,' Mary greeted him as he passed her in the corridor.

'Morning,' Tobias replied, but he watched her more closely than he ever had before.

The middle aged woman looked harmless enough. She was short and stocky, and walked with a slight limp. Her curly black hair framed a soft face and her smile always appeared friendly. Now though, Tobias couldn't help but wonder if the smile hid a dark secret or if the limp was even real. Could Mary be the Wraith?

'Have a good day at school honey,' she called after him as he stepped into the stairwell.

'Thanks,' Tobias called back.

He was trying his best to sound and look cheerful, but when the door shut behind him, a shudder ran up his spine which was so severe it caused his shoulders to tense up.

'I hate not knowing who the Wraith might be,' he told Hex.

'That is understandable. But we will find them.'

'I hope so.'

Reaching the bottom of the stairs Tobias pulled open the main doors of the apartment block and stepped out into the cold morning air. Jay and Kayt were already waiting for him outside and they rushed over as soon as they saw him.

'Hey bestie,' Kayt greeted him with a big hug around his neck. 'You look like you are doing good.'

'Yeah,' Jay added. 'You would have no idea that you nearly died the other day.'

'Erm, thanks. I think.' Tobias replied.

'My dad always says, whatever doesn't kill you makes you stronger.' Kayt practically skipped along as she spoke but Jay stopped and looked confused.

'That makes absolutely no sense,' he said. 'What if you get hit by a truck and it breaks all your bones but you don't die? That wouldn't make you stronger.'

'It might make you stronger mentally,' Kayt replied.

'So it would turn you into a nerd or something?'

'No, I mean you might develop the emotional strength to overcome your handicap.'

'I guess. Personally, I would prefer to just not get hit by the truck.'

'Well, yes, obviously. But I assumed that wasn't an option in your example.'

Jay just shrugged in response to Kayt and she let out a deep sigh before turning to face Tobias.

 'Have you had any more thoughts on who the Wraith might be?'

'I have no idea who it could be,' Tobias admitted.

'What if the Wraith is a woman?' Jay asked.

'What would be wrong with it being a woman?' Kayt replied. She shot him a sideways glance which challenged him to say something negative.

'Nothing. I mean, women can be evil monsters too I guess. I just mean if it is a woman, what about Hex? Would he want to be a woman?'

'I hadn't considered such an eventuality,' Hex admitted. 'But the boy does raise an interesting question. I would say that, at this point, I would be happy with anybody as long as it meant I was free of this cursed stone.'

'That's fair,' Jay responded, then as if it was a deep and meaningful thought, he added, 'let's just hope she isn't some old biddy.'

Kayt punched him in the shoulder.

'Hey! What was that for?'

'You can be such an idiot.'

Tobias dropped back and let the two of them walk on ahead. He had no idea who the Wraith was or how he was going to handle the conflict bubbling up inside of himself. But as he watched Jay and Kayt laughing together, he felt at peace.

No matter what happened now, he had friends. He was certain that it would all be okay.

Epilogue

The Wraith watched the three children from the shadows of a narrow alleyway. Tobias Crow had to be its priority but it also sensed something special in the other two. Maybe it was because they had been to the Realms, or maybe it was their proximity to Tobias. Regardless, it would enjoy destroying them and that thought brought a delighted sneer to its lips.

A soft purr announced the arrival of another presence in the alley which moved out of the darkness and stood by the Wraith's side. The Wraith reached down to pat the Shadow Hunter behind the ears. Though it clearly enjoyed the attention and it pushed its head harder into the Wraiths hand, the Shadow Hunter's one good eye never left the three children. The deep scar where its left eye had once been continued to seep a pale red fluid.

The Shadow Hunter growled angrily.

In response, the Wraith took hold of the scruff of its neck and pulled back hard. 'Not yet,' the Wraith warned. 'They cut us off when they destroyed the Gate. But I have a plan. We must be patient.'

The Shadow Hunter pulled itself free of the Wraiths grip and growled angrily. Still, it did as it was told and stayed where it was.

'Do not worry,' the Wraith said. 'You will have your revenge, but I want to play for a bit first. Now, gather the rest of your pack. We have work to do.'

Tobias Crow will return in Book 3 of

The Saga of Tobias Crow,

Greed's Revenge

In the meantime, you can find

more from P.S. Osborne at;

www.psosborne.com

Acknowledgements

As always, there are far too many people who deserve recognition than I could possibly fit on just a couple of pages. Of course my family sits firmly at the top of this list and deserves more praise than I could ever give. My son has inspired me every day, my mum has been an endless source of strength and support, and by not descending into a murderous rage, my Wife has once again displayed a patience which I am not entirely certain I deserve.

My friends have also provided immeasurable support and for the first time I can also give a huge thank you to all my fans who purchased book 1 and have waited patiently for book 2. I never thought that I would be lucky enough to actually have fans but you have all been amazing.

Finally, a special thank you also goes out to Mark Dobson for his spectacular illustrations, and Design for Writers who continue to produce phenomenal covers.

Printed in Great Britain
by Amazon